Acclaim for

The House on Mango Street by **Sandra Cisneros**

"*The House on Mango Street* is so succinct, funny, and beautiful that it is timeless. It's poetry and song with yearning and love that we can all recognize. It's one of those books that we will be reading and rereading for a very long time." —Edwidge Danticat

"Sandra Cisneros has made a difference to Latino literature; beginning with *House on Mango Street,* her works have conveyed the Southwestern Latino experience with verve, charm, and passion." —Oscar Hijuelos

"*The House on Mango Street* is a book that will be cherished for generations. With its tenderness, its humor, and its wide-eyed truth telling, Esperanza's story becomes *our* story, whether we're Latinas or not." —Cristina García

"Brilliant. . . . [Cisneros's] work is sensitive, alert, nuanceful. . . . Rich with music and picture." —Gwendolyn Brooks

"*The House on Mango Street* has given a voice to all of us who have made the United States home, while never forgetting where we come from. . . . An unforgettable and indispensable book." —Jorge Ramos

"Sandra and her *House* are all things—the house, a home; the mango, a fruit; the street, a way, all in one." —Eduardo Galeano

"*The House on Mango Street* was the sort of reality-altering book that broke it all open for me. Sandra Cisneros has a voice with character, gusto, and chiseled craft. It didn't just reach out to me becau reaching out to touch ever ary history."

Sandra Cisneros

The House on Mango Street

Sandra Cisneros is a poet, short story writer, novelist, and essayist whose numerous awards include NEA fellowships in both poetry and fiction, the Texas Medal of Arts, a MacArthur Fellowship, several honorary doctorates, and national and international book awards, including Chicago's Fifth Star Award, the PEN Center USA Literary Award, and the PEN/Nabokov Award for Achievement in International Literature. She is the recipient of the Ford Foundation's Art of Change Fellowship, was recognized among The Frederick Douglass 200, and was awarded the National Medal of Arts by President Obama in 2016.

Cisneros is the author of two novels, *The House on Mango Street* and *Caramelo*; a collection of short stories, *Woman Hollering Creek*; two books of poetry, *My Wicked Wicked Ways* and *Loose Woman*; a children's book, *Hairs/Pelitos*; a selected anthology of her own work, *Vintage Cisneros*; an autobiography, *A House of My Own*; and, with Ester Hernández, *Have You Seen Marie?*, a fable for adults. She is the founder of the Macondo Foundation, an association of writers united to serve underserved communities.

www.sandracisneros.com

The House on Mango Street

Sandra Cisneros

Vintage Contemporaries
Vintage Books
A Division of Penguin Random House LLC
New York

SECOND VINTAGE CONTEMPORARIES EDITION, FEBRUARY 2009

Library of Congress Cataloging-in-Publication Data
Cisneros, Sandra.
The house on Mango Street / by Sandra Cisneros.
p. cm.
"Originally published by Arte Público Press in 1984"—T.p. verso.
I. Title.
PS3553.I78H6 1991
813'.54—dc20 90-50593
CIP

Vintage Contemporaries Trade Paperback ISBN: 978-0-679-73477-2
eBook ISBN: 978-0-345-80719-9

Author photograph (introduction) © Diana Solis
Book design by Cathryn S. Aison

www.vintagebooks.com

Printed in the United States of America
120 119 118 117 116 115 114

A las Mujeres
To the Women

Contents

A House of My Own

The young woman in this photograph is me when I was writing *The House on Mango Street*. She's in her office, a room that had probably been a child's bedroom when families lived in this apartment. It has no door and is only slightly wider than the walk-in pantry. But it has great light and sits above the hallway door downstairs, so she can hear her neighbors come and go. She's posed as if she's just looked up from her work for a moment, but in real life she never writes in this office. She writes in the kitchen, the only room with a heater.

It's Chicago, 1980, in the down-at-the-heels Bucktown neighborhood before it's discovered by folks with money. The young woman lives at 1814 N. Paulina Street second floor front. Nelson Algren once wandered these streets. Saul Bellow's turf was over on Division Street, walking distance away. It's a neighborhood that reeks of beer and urine, of sausage and beans.

The young woman fills her "office" with things she drags home from the flea market at Maxwell Street. Antique typewriters, alphabet blocks, asparagus ferns, bookshelves, ceramic figurines from Occupied Japan, wicker baskets, birdcages, hand-painted photos. Things she likes to look at. It's important to have this space to look and think. When she lived at home, the things she looked at scolded her and made her feel sad and depressed. They said, "Wash me." They said, "Lazy." They said, "You ought." But the things in her office are magical and invite her to play. They fill her with light. It's the room where she can be quiet and still and listen to the voices inside herself. She likes being alone in the daytime.

As a girl, she dreamed about having a silent home, just to herself, the way other women dreamed of their weddings. Instead of collecting lace and linen for her trousseau, the young woman buys old things from the thrift stores on grimy Milwaukee Avenue for her future house-of-her-own—faded quilts, cracked vases, chipped saucers, lamps in need of love.

The young woman returned to Chicago after graduate school and moved back into her father's house, 1754 N. Keeler, back into her girl's room with its twin bed and floral wallpaper. She was twenty-three and a half. Now she summoned her courage and told her father she wanted to live alone again, like she did when she was away at school. He looked at her with that eye of the rooster before it attacks, but she wasn't alarmed. She'd seen that look before and knew he was harmless. She was his favorite, and it was only a matter of waiting.

The daughter claimed she'd been taught that a writer needs quiet, privacy, and long stretches of solitude to think. The father decided too much college and too many gringo friends had ruined her. In a way he was right. In a way she was right. When she thinks to herself in her father's language, she knows sons and daughters don't leave their parents' house until they marry. When she thinks in English, she knows she should've been on her own since eighteen.

For a time father and daughter reached a truce. She agreed to move into the basement of a building where the oldest of her six brothers and his wife lived, 4832 W. Homer. But after a few months, when the big brother upstairs turned out to be Big Brother, she got on her bicycle and rode through the neighborhood of her high school days until she spotted an apartment with fresh-painted walls and masking tape on the windows. Then she knocked on the storefront downstairs. That's how she convinced the landlord she was his new tenant.

Her father can't understand why she wants to live in a hundred-year-old building with big windows that let in the cold. She knows her apartment is clean, but the hallway is scuffed and scary, though she and the woman upstairs take turns mopping it regularly. The hall needs paint, and there's nothing they can do about that. When the father visits, he climbs up the stairs muttering with disgust. Inside, he looks at her books arranged in milk crates, at the futon on the floor in a bedroom with no door, and whispers, "Hippie," in the same way he looks at boys hanging out in his neighborhood and says, *"Drogas."* When he sees the space heater in the kitchen, the father shakes his head and sighs, "Why did I work so hard to buy a house with a furnace so she could go backwards and live like this?"

When she's alone, she savors her apartment of high ceilings and windows that let in the sky, the new carpeting and walls white as typing paper, the walk-in pantry with empty shelves, her bedroom without a door, her office with its typewriter, and the big front-room windows with their view of a street, rooftops, trees, and the dizzy traffic of the Kennedy Expressway.

Between her building and the brick wall of the next is a tidy, sunken garden. The only people who ever enter the garden are a family who speak like guitars, a family with a Southern accent. At dusk they appear with a pet monkey in a cage and sit on a green bench and talk and laugh. She spies on them from behind her bedroom curtains and wonders where they got the monkey.

Her father calls every week to say, "*Mija*, when are you coming home?" What does her mother say about all this? She puts her hands on her hips and boasts, "She gets it from me." When the father is in the room, the mother just shrugs and says, "What can I do?" The mother doesn't object. She knows what it is to live a life filled with regrets, and she doesn't want her daughter to live that life too. She always supported the daughter's projects, so long as she went to school. The mother who painted the walls of their Chicago homes the color of flowers; who planted tomatoes and roses in her garden; sang arias; practiced solos on her son's drum set; boogied along with the *Soul Train* dancers; glued travel posters on her kitchen wall with Karo syrup; herded her kids weekly to the library, to public concerts, to museums; wore a button on her lapel that said "Feed the People Not the Pentagon"; who never went beyond the ninth grade. *That* mother. She nudges her daughter and says, "Good lucky you studied."

The father wants his daughter to be a weather girl on television, or to marry and have babies. She doesn't want to be a TV weather girl. Nor does she want to marry and have babies. Not yet. Maybe later, but there are so many other things she must do in her lifetime first. Travel. Learn how to dance the tango. Publish a book. Live in other cities. Win a National Endowment for the Arts award. See the Northern Lights. Jump out of a cake.

She stares at the ceilings and walls of her apartment the way she once stared at the ceilings and walls of the apartments she grew up in, inventing pictures in the cracks in the plaster, inventing stories to go with these pictures. At night, under the circle of light from a cheap metal lamp clamped to the kitchen table, she sits with paper and a pen and pretends she's not afraid. She's trying to live like a writer.

Where she gets these ideas about living like a writer, she has no clue. She hasn't read Virginia Woolf yet. She doesn't know about Rosario Castellanos or Sor Juana Inés de la Cruz. Gloria Anzaldúa and Cherríe Moraga are cutting their own paths through the world somewhere, but she doesn't know about them. She doesn't know anything. She's making things up as she goes.

When the photo of the young woman who was me was snapped, I still called myself a poet, though I'd been writing stories since grammar school. I'd gravitated back to fiction while in the Iowa poetry workshop. Poetry, as it was taught at Iowa, was a house of cards, a tower of ideas, but I can't communicate an idea except through a story.

The woman I am in the photo was working on a series of vignettes, little by little, along with her poetry. I already had a title—*The House on Mango Street*. Fifty pages had been written, but I still didn't think of it as a novel. It was just a jar of buttons, like the mismatched embroidered pillowcases and monogrammed napkins I tugged from the bins at the Goodwill. I wrote these things and thought of them as "little stories," though I sensed they were connected to each other. I hadn't heard of story cycles yet. I hadn't read Ermilo Abreu Gómez's *Canek*, Elena Poniatowska's *Lilus Kikus*, Gwendolyn Brooks' *Maud Martha*, Nellie Campobello's *My Mother's Hands*. That would come later, when I had more time and solitude to read.

The woman I once was wrote the first three stories of *House* in one weekend at Iowa. But because I wasn't in the fiction workshop, they wouldn't count toward my MFA thesis. I didn't argue; my thesis advisor reminded me too much of my father. I worked on these little stories on the side for comfort when I wasn't writing poetry for credit. I shared them with colleagues like poet Joy Harjo, who was also having a hard time in the poetry workshops, and fiction writer Dennis Mathis, a small-town Illinois native, but whose paperback library was from the world.

Little-little stories were in literary vogue at the time, in the '70s. Dennis told me about the Japanese Nobel Prize winner Kawabata's minimal "palm of the hand" stories. We fried omelets for dinner and read García Márquez and Heinrich Böll stories aloud. We both preferred experimental writers—all men back then except for Grace Paley—rebels like ourselves. Dennis would become a lifelong editor, ally, and voice on the phone when either one of us lost heart.

The young woman in the photo is modeling her book-in-progress after *Dream Tigers* by Jorge Luis Borges— a writer she'd read since high school, story fragments that ring like Hans Christian Andersen, or Ovid, or entries from the encyclopedia. She wants to write stories that ignore borders between genres, between written and spoken, between highbrow literature and children's nursery rhymes, between New York and the imaginary village of Macondo, between the U.S. and Mexico. It's true, she wants the writers she admires to respect her work, but she also wants people who don't usually read books to enjoy these stories too. She *doesn't* want to write a book that a reader won't understand and would feel ashamed for not understanding.

She thinks stories are about beauty. Beauty that is there to be admired by anyone, like a herd of clouds grazing overhead. She thinks people who are busy working for a living deserve beautiful little stories, because they don't have much time and are often tired. She has in mind a book that can be opened at any page and will still make sense to the reader who doesn't know what came before or comes after.

She experiments, creating a text that is as succinct and flexible as poetry, snapping sentences into fragments so that the reader pauses, making each sentence serve *her* and not the other way round, abandoning quotation marks to streamline the typography and make the page as simple and readable as possible. So that the sentences are pliant as branches and can be read in more ways than one.

Sometimes the woman I once was goes out on weekends to meet with other writers. Sometimes I invite these friends to come to my apartment to workshop each other's work. We come from Black, white, Latino communities. We are men and we are women. What we have in common is our sense that art should serve our communities. Together we publish an anthology—*Emergency Tacos*—because we finish our collaborations in the early hours before dawn and gather at the same twenty-four-hour *taquería* on Belmont Avenue, like a multicultural version of Hopper's *Nighthawks* painting. The *Emergency Tacos* writers organize monthly arts events at my brother Keek's apartment—

Galeria Quique. We do this with no capital except our valuable time. We do this because the world we live in is a house on fire and the people we love are burning.

The young woman in the photograph gets up in the morning to go to the job that pays the rent on her Paulina Street apartment. She teaches at a school in Pilsen, her mother's old neighborhood on Chicago's south side, a Mexican neighborhood where the rent is cheap and too many families live crowded together. Landlords and the city take no responsibility for the rats, trash that isn't collected often enough, porches that collapse, apartments without fire escapes, until a tragedy happens and several people die. Then they hold investigations for a little while, but the problems go on until the next death, the next investigation, the next bout of forgetting.

The young woman works with students who have dropped out of high school but have decided to try again for their diplomas. She learns from her students that they have more difficult lives than her storyteller's imagination can invent. Her life has been comfortable and privileged compared to theirs. She never had to worry about feeding her babies before she went to class. She never had a father or boyfriend who beat her at night and left her bruised in the morning. She didn't have to plan an alternative route to avoid gangs in the school hallway. Her parents didn't plead with her to drop out of school so she could help them earn money.

How can art make a difference in the world? This was never asked at Iowa. Should she be teaching these students to write poetry when they need to know how to defend themselves from someone beating them up? Can a memoir by Malcolm X or a novel by García Márquez save them from the daily blows? And what about those who have such learning problems they can't even manage a book by Dr. Seuss, but can weave a spoken story so wondrous, she wants to take notes. Should she give up writing and study something useful like medicine? How can she teach her students to take control of their own destiny? She loves these students. What should she be doing to save their lives?

The young woman's teaching job leads to the next, and now she finds herself a counselor/recruiter at her alma mater, Loyola University on the north side, in Rogers Park. I have health benefits. I don't bring work home anymore. My work day ends at five p.m. Now I have evenings free to do my own work. I feel like a real writer.

At the university I work for a program that no longer exists, the Educational Opportunity Program, that assists "disadvantaged" students. It's in keeping with my philosophy, and I can still help the students from my previous job. But when my most brilliant student is accepted, enrolls, and drops out in her first semester, I collapse on my desk from grief, from exhaustion, and feel like dropping out myself.

I write about my students because I don't know what else to do with their stories. Writing them down allows me to sleep.

On the weekends, if I can sidestep guilt and avoid my father's demands to come home for Sunday dinner, I'm free to stay home and write. I feel like a bad daughter ignoring my father, but I feel worse when I don't write. Either way, I never feel completely happy.

One Saturday the woman at the typewriter accepts an invitation to a literary soiree. But when she arrives, she feels she's made a terrible mistake. All the writers are old men. She has been invited by Leon Forrest, a Black novelist who was trying to be kind and invite more women, more people-of-color, but so far, she's the only woman, and he and she the only coloreds.

She's there because she's the author of a new book of poetry—*Bad Boys* from Mango Press, the literary efforts of Gary Soto and Lorna Dee Cervantes. Her book is four pages long and was bound together on a kitchen table with a stapler and a spoon. Many of the other guests, she soon realizes, have written *real* books, hardbacks from big New York houses, printed in editions of hundreds of thousands on actual presses. Is she really a writer or is she only pretending to be a writer?

The guest of honor is a famous writer who went to the Iowa Workshop several years before she got there. His latest book has just been sold to Hollywood. He speaks and carries himself as if he's the Emperor of Everything.

At the end of the evening, she finds herself searching for a ride home. She came on the bus, and the Emperor offers to give her a lift home. But she's not going home, she's got her heart set on a movie that's showing only tonight. She's afraid of going to the movies alone, and that's why she's decided to go. Because she's afraid.

The famous writer drives a sports car. The seats smell of leather, and the dashboard is lit like an airplane cockpit. Her own car doesn't always start and has a hole in the floor near the accelerator that lets in rain and snow, so she has to wear boots when she drives. The famous writer talks and talks, but she can't hear what he is saying, because her own thoughts are drowning him out like a wind. She doesn't say anything, doesn't have to. She is just young and pretty enough to feed the famous writer's ego by nodding enthusiastically at everything he says until he drops her off in front of the cinema. She hopes the famous writer notices she is going to see *Gentlemen Prefer Blondes* alone. To tell the truth, she feels miserable walking up to the box office by herself, but she forces herself to buy the ticket and go in because she loves this movie.

The theater is packed. It feels to the young woman as if everybody is there with somebody, except her. Finally, the scene where Marilyn sings "Diamonds Are a Girl's Best Friend." The colors are cartoon-wonderful, the set deliciously campy, the lyrics clever, the whole number is pure old-style glamour. Marilyn is sensational. After her song is over, the audience breaks into applause as if this were a live performance, though sad Marilyn has been dead years and years.

The woman who is me goes home proud of having gone to the movies alone. *See? It wasn't that difficult.* But as she bolts the door of her apartment, she bursts into tears. "I don't have diamonds," she sobs, not knowing what she means, except she knows even then it's not about diamonds. Every few weeks, she has a messy crying jag like this that leaves her feeling shipwrecked and awful. It's such a regular occurrence she thinks these storms of depression are as normal as rain.

What is the woman in the photograph afraid of? She's afraid of walking from her parked car to her apartment in the dark. She's afraid of the scuffling sounds in the walls. She's afraid she'll fall in love and get stuck living in Chicago. She's afraid of ghosts, deep water, rodents, night, things that move too fast—cars, airplanes, her life. She's afraid she'll have to move back home again if she isn't brave enough to live alone.

Throughout all this, I am writing stories to go with that title, *The House on Mango Street.* Sometimes I write about people I remember, sometimes I write about people

I've just met, often I mix the two together. My students from Pilsen who sat before me when I was teaching, with girls who sat beside me in another classroom a decade before. I pick up parts of Bucktown, like the monkey garden next door, and plop it down in the Humboldt Park block where I lived during my middle and high school years—1525 N. Campbell Street.

Often all I have is a title with no story—"The Family of Little Feet,"—and I have to make the title kick me in the behind to get me going. Or, sometimes all I've got is a first sentence—"You can never have too much sky." One of my Pilsen students said I had said this, and she never forgot it. Good thing she remembered and quoted it back to me. "They came with the wind that blows in August . . ." This line came to me in a dream. Sometimes the best ideas come in dreams. Sometimes the worst ideas come from there, too!

Whether the idea came from a sentence I heard buzzing around somewhere and saved in a jar, or from a title I picked up and pocketed, the stories always insist on telling me where they want to end. They often surprise me by stopping when I had every intention of galloping along a little further. They're stubborn. They know best when there's no more to be said. The last sentence must ring like the final notes at the end of a mariachi song— *tan-tán*—to tell you when the song is done.

The people I wrote about were real, for the most part, from here and there, now and then, but sometimes three real people would be braided together into one made-up person. Usually when I thought I was creating someone from my imagination, it turned out I was remembering someone I'd forgotten or someone standing so close I couldn't see her at all.

I cut apart and stitched together events to tailor the

story, gave it shape so it had a beginning, middle, and end, because real life stories rarely come to us complete. Emotions, though, can't be invented, can't be borrowed. All the emotions my characters feel, good or bad, are mine.

I meet Norma Alarcón. She is to become one of my earliest publishers and my lifetime friend. The first time she walks through the rooms of the apartment on North Paulina, she notices the quiet rooms, the collection of typewriters, the books and Japanese figurines, the windows with the view of freeway and sky. She walks as if on tiptoe, peering into every room, even the pantry and closet as if looking for something. "You live here . . ." she asks, "alone?"

"Yes."

"So . . ." She pauses. "How did you do it?"

Norma, I did it by doing the things I was afraid of doing so that I would no longer be afraid. Moving away to go to graduate school. Traveling abroad alone. Earning my own money and living by myself. Posing as an author when I was afraid, just as I posed in that photo you used on the first cover of *Third Woman*.

And, finally, when I was ready, after I had apprenticed with professional writers over several years, partnering with the right agent. My father, who sighed and wished for me to marry, was, at the end of his life, much more gratified I had my agent Susan Bergholz providing for me rather than a husband. *¿Ha llamado Susan?* he asked me daily, because if Susan called it meant good news. Diamonds may do for a girl, but an agent is a woman writer's best friend.

I couldn't trust my own voice, Norma. People saw a little girl when they looked at me and heard a little girl's voice when I spoke. Because I was unsure of my own adult voice and often censored myself, I made up another voice, Esperanza's, to be my voice and ask the things I needed answers to myself—"Which way?" I didn't know exactly, but I knew which routes I didn't want to take—Sally, Rafaela, Ruthie—women whose lives were white crosses on the roadside.

At Iowa we never talked about serving others with our writing. It was all about serving ourselves. But there were no other examples to follow until you introduced me to Mexican writers Sor Juana Inés de la Cruz, Elena Poniatowska, Elena Garro, Rosario Castellanos. The young woman in the photograph was looking for another way to be— *"otro modo de ser,"* as Castellanos put it.

Until you brought us all together as U.S. Latina writers—Cherríe Moraga, Gloria Anzaldúa, Marjorie Agosín, Carla Trujillo, Diana Solís, Sandra María Esteves, Diane Gómez, Salima Rivera, Margarita López, Beatriz Badikian, Carmen Abrego, Denise Chávez, Helena Viramontes— until then, Normita, we had no idea what we were doing was extraordinary.

I no longer make Chicago my home, but Chicago still makes its home in me. I have Chicago stories I have yet to write. So long as those stories kick inside me, Chicago will still be home.

Eventually I took a job in San Antonio. Left. Came back. And left again. I kept coming back lured by cheap rent. Affordable housing is essential to an artist. I could, in time, even buy my own first house, a hundred-year-old home once periwinkle, but now painted a Mexican pink.

Two years ago my office went up in my backyard, a building created from my Mexican memories. I am writing this today from this very office, Mexican marigold on the outside, morning-glory violet on the inside. Wind chimes ring from the terrace. Trains moan in the distance all the time, ours is a neighborhood of trains. The same San Antonio River tourists know from the Riverwalk wends its way behind my house to the Missions and beyond until it empties into the Gulf of Mexico. From my terrace you can see the river where it bends into an S.

White cranes float across the sky like a scene painted on a lacquered screen. The river shares the land with ducks, raccoons, possums, skunks, buzzards, butterflies, hawks, turtles, snakes, owls, even though we're walking distance to downtown. And within the confines of my own garden there are plenty of other creatures too—yappy dogs, kamikaze cats, one lovesick parrot with a crush on me.

This is my house.

Bliss.

October 24th, 2007. You come down from Chicago for a visit, Mama. You don't want to come. I make you come. You don't like to leave your house anymore, your back hurts you say, but I insist. I built this office beside the river for you as much as for me, and I want you to see it.

Once, years ago, you telephoned and said in an urgent voice, "When are you going to build your office? I just saw Isabel Allende on PBS and she has a HUGE desk and a BIG office." You were upset because I was writing on the kitchen table again like in the old days.

And now here we are, on the rooftop of a saffron building with a river view, a space all my own just to write.

We climb up to the room I work in, above the library, and out to the balcony facing the river.

You have to rest. There are industrial buildings on the opposite bank—abandoned granaries and silos—but they're so rain-rusted and sun-bleached, they have their own charm, like public sculptures. When you've recovered your breath, we continue.

I'm especially proud of the spiral staircase to the rooftop. I'd always dreamed of having one, just like the houses in Mexico. Even the word for them in Spanish is wonderful—*un caracol*—a snail. Our footsteps clang on each metal step, the dogs following so close we have to scold them.

"Your office is bigger than in the pictures you sent," you say delighted. I imagine you're comparing it to Isabel Allende's.

"Where did you get the drapes in the library? I bet they cost a pretty penny. Too bad your brothers couldn't upholster your chairs for you and save you some money. Boy, this place is niiiiice!" you say, your voice sliding up the scales like a river grackle.

I plop yoga mats on the rooftop, and we sit cross-legged to watch the sun descend. We drink your favorite, Italian sparkling wine, to celebrate your arrival, to celebrate my office.

The sky absorbs the night quickly-quickly, dissolving into the color of a plum. I lie on my back and watch clouds scurry past in a hurry to get home. Stars come out shyly, one by one. You lie down next to me and drape one leg over mine like when we sleep together at your home. We always sleep together when I'm there. At first because there isn't any other bed. But later, after Papa dies, just because you want me near. It's the only time you let yourself be affectionate.

"What if we invite everybody down here for Christmas next year?" I ask, "What do you think?"

"We'll see," you say lost in your own thoughts.

The moon climbs the front yard mesquite tree, leaps over the terrace ledge and astonishes us. It's a full moon, a huge nimbus like the prints of Yoshitoshi. From here on, I won't be able to see a full moon again without thinking of you, this moment. But right now, I don't know this.

You close your eyes. You look like you're sleeping. The plane ride must've tired you. "Good lucky you studied," you say without opening your eyes. You mean my office, my life.

I say to you, "Good lucky."

For my mother, Elvira Cordero Cisneros
July llth, 1929–November lst, 2007

May 26th, 2008
Casa Xóchitl, San Antonio de Béxar, Texas

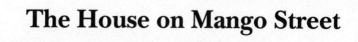

The House on Mango Street

The
House
on
Mango Street

We didn't always live on Mango Street. Before that
we lived on Loomis on the third floor, and before that we
lived on Keeler. Before Keeler it was Paulina, and before
that I can't remember. But what I remember most is moving a lot. Each time it seemed there'd be one more of us.
By the time we got to Mango Street we were six—Mama,
Papa, Carlos, Kiki, my sister Nenny and me.

The house on Mango Street is ours, and we don't have
to pay rent to anybody, or share the yard with the people
downstairs, or be careful not to make too much noise, and
there isn't a landlord banging on the ceiling with a broom.
But even so, it's not the house we'd thought we'd get.

We had to leave the flat on Loomis quick. The water pipes broke and the landlord wouldn't fix them because the house was too old. We had to leave fast. We were using the washroom next door and carrying water over in empty milk gallons. That's why Mama and Papa looked for a house, and that's why we moved into the house on Mango Street, far away, on the other side of town.

They always told us that one day we would move into a house, a real house that would be ours for always so we wouldn't have to move each year. And our house would have running water and pipes that worked. And inside it would have real stairs, not hallway stairs, but stairs inside like the houses on T.V. And we'd have a basement and at least three washrooms so when we took a bath we wouldn't have to tell everybody. Our house would be white with trees around it, a great big yard and grass growing without a fence. This was the house Papa talked about when he held a lottery ticket and this was the house Mama dreamed up in the stories she told us before we went to bed.

But the house on Mango Street is not the way they told it at all. It's small and red with tight steps in front and windows so small you'd think they were holding their breath. Bricks are crumbling in places, and the front door is so swollen you have to push hard to get in. There is no front yard, only four little elms the city planted by the curb. Out back is a small garage for the car we don't own yet and a small yard that looks smaller between the two buildings on either side. There are stairs in our house, but they're ordinary hallway stairs, and the house has only one washroom. Everybody has to share a bedroom—Mama and Papa, Carlos and Kiki, me and Nenny.

Once when we were living on Loomis, a nun from my school passed by and saw me playing out front. The laundromat downstairs had been boarded up because it had been robbed two days before and the owner had painted on the wood YES WE'RE OPEN so as not to lose business.

Where do you live? she asked.

There, I said pointing up to the third floor.

You live *there*?

There. I had to look to where she pointed—the third floor, the paint peeling, wooden bars Papa had nailed on the windows so we wouldn't fall out. You live *there*? The way she said it made me feel like nothing. *There.* I lived *there.* I nodded.

I knew then I had to have a house. A real house. One I could point to. But this isn't it. The house on Mango Street isn't it. For the time being, Mama says. Temporary, says Papa. But I know how those things go.

Hairs

Everybody in our family has different hair. My Papa's hair is like a broom, all up in the air. And me, my hair is lazy. It never obeys barrettes or bands. Carlos' hair is thick and straight. He doesn't need to comb it. Nenny's hair is slippery—slides out of your hand. And Kiki, who is the youngest, has hair like fur.

But my mother's hair, my mother's hair, like little rosettes, like little candy circles all curly and pretty because she pinned it in pincurls all day, sweet to put your nose into when she is holding you, holding you and you feel safe, is the warm smell of bread before you bake it, is the smell when she makes room for you on her side of the bed still warm with her skin, and you sleep near her, the rain outside falling and Papa snoring. The snoring, the rain, and Mama's hair that smells like bread.

Boys & Girls

The boys and the girls live in separate worlds. The boys in their universe and we in ours. My brothers for example. They've got plenty to say to me and Nenny inside the house. But outside they can't be seen talking to girls. Carlos and Kiki are each other's best friend . . . not ours.

Nenny is too young to be my friend. She's just my sister and that was not my fault. You don't pick your sisters, you just get them and sometimes they come like Nenny.

She can't play with those Vargas kids or she'll turn out just like them. And since she comes right after me, she is my responsibility.

Someday I will have a best friend all my own. One I can tell my secrets to. One who will understand my jokes without my having to explain them. Until then I am a red balloon, a balloon tied to an anchor.

My Name

In English my name means hope. In Spanish it means too many letters. It means sadness, it means waiting. It is like the number nine. A muddy color. It is the Mexican records my father plays on Sunday mornings when he is shaving, songs like sobbing.

It was my great-grandmother's name and now it is mine. She was a horse woman too, born like me in the Chinese year of the horse—which is supposed to be bad luck if you're born female—but I think this is a Chinese lie because the Chinese, like the Mexicans, don't like their women strong.

My great-grandmother. I would've liked to have

known her, a wild horse of a woman, so wild she wouldn't marry. Until my great-grandfather threw a sack over her head and carried her off. Just like that, as if she were a fancy chandelier. That's the way he did it.

And the story goes she never forgave him. She looked out the window her whole life, the way so many women sit their sadness on an elbow. I wonder if she made the best with what she got or was she sorry because she couldn't be all the things she wanted to be. Esperanza. I have inherited her name, but I don't want to inherit her place by the window.

At school they say my name funny as if the syllables were made out of tin and hurt the roof of your mouth. But in Spanish my name is made out of a softer something, like silver, not quite as thick as sister's name—Magdalena—which is uglier than mine. Magdalena who at least can come home and become Nenny. But I am always Esperanza.

I would like to baptize myself under a new name, a name more like the real me, the one nobody sees. Esperanza as Lisandra or Maritza or Zeze the X. Yes. Something like Zeze the X will do.

Cathy
Queen of Cats

She says, I am the great great grand cousin of the queen of France. She lives upstairs, over there, next door to Joe the baby-grabber. Keep away from him, she says. He is full of danger. Benny and Blanca own the corner store. They're okay except don't lean on the candy counter. Two girls raggedy as rats live across the street. You don't want to know them. Edna is the lady who owns the building next to you. She used to own a building big as a whale, but her brother sold it. Their mother said no, no, don't ever sell it. I won't. And then she closed her eyes and he sold it. Alicia is stuck-up ever since she went to college. She used to like me but now she doesn't.

Cathy who is queen of cats has cats and cats and cats. Baby cats, big cats, skinny cats, sick cats. Cats asleep like little donuts. Cats on top of the refrigerator. Cats taking a walk on the dinner table. Her house is like cat heaven.

You want a friend, she says. Okay, I'll be your friend. But only till next Tuesday. That's when we move away. Got to. Then as if she forgot I just moved in, she says the neighborhood is getting bad.

Cathy's father will have to fly to France one day and find her great great distant grand cousin on her father's side and inherit the family house. How do I know this is so? She told me so. In the meantime they'll just have to move a little farther north from Mango Street, a little farther away every time people like us keep moving in.

Our Good Day

If you give me five dollars I will be your friend forever. That's what the little one tells me.

Five dollars is cheap since I don't have any friends
except Cathy who is only my friend till Tuesday.

Five dollars, five dollars.

She is trying to get somebody to chip in so they can
buy a bicycle from this kid named Tito. They already have
ten dollars and all they need is five more.

Only five dollars, she says.

Don't talk to them, says Cathy. Can't you see they smell
like a broom.

But I like them. Their clothes are crooked and old.

They are wearing shiny Sunday shoes without socks. It makes their bald ankles all red, but I like them. Especially the big one who laughs with all her teeth. I like her even though she lets the little one do all the talking.

Five dollars, the little one says, only five.

Cathy is tugging my arm and I know whatever I do next will make her mad forever.

Wait a minute, I say, and run inside to get the five dollars. I have three dollars saved and I take two of Nenny's. She's not home, but I'm sure she'll be glad when she finds out we own a bike. When I get back, Cathy is gone like I knew she would be, but I don't care. I have two new friends and a bike too.

My name is Lucy, the big one says. This here is Rachel my sister.

I'm her sister, says Rachel. Who are you?

And I wish my name was Cassandra or Alexis or Maritza—anything but Esperanza—but when I tell them my name they don't laugh.

We come from Texas, Lucy says and grins. Her was born here, but me I'm Texas.

You mean *she,* I say.

No, I'm from Texas, and doesn't get it.

This bike is three ways ours, says Rachel who is thinking ahead already. Mine today, Lucy's tomorrow and yours day after.

But everybody wants to ride it today because the bike is new, so we decide to take turns *after* tomorrow. Today it belongs to all of us.

I don't tell them about Nenny just yet. It's too complicated. Especially since Rachel almost put out Lucy's eye about who was going to get to ride it first. But finally we agree to ride it together. Why not?

Because Lucy has long legs she pedals. I sit on the

back seat and Rachel is skinny enough to get up on the handlebars which makes the bike all wobbly as if the wheels are spaghetti, but after a bit you get used to it.

We ride fast and faster. Past my house, sad and red and crumbly in places, past Mr. Benny's grocery on the corner, and down the avenue which is dangerous. Laundromat, junk store, drugstore, windows and cars and more cars, and around the block back to Mango.

People on the bus wave. A very fat lady crossing the street says, You sure got quite a load there.

Rachel shouts, You got quite a load there too. She is very sassy.

Down, down Mango Street we go. Rachel, Lucy, me. Our new bicycle. Laughing the crooked ride back.

Laughter

Nenny and I don't look like sisters . . . not right away. Not the way you can tell with Rachel and Lucy who have the same fat popsicle lips like everybody else in their family. But me and Nenny, we are more alike than you would know. Our laughter for example. Not the shy ice cream bells' giggle of Rachel and Lucy's family, but all of a sudden and surprised like a pile of dishes breaking. And other things I can't explain.

One day we were passing a house that looked, in my mind, like houses I had seen in Mexico. I don't know why. There was nothing about the house that looked exactly like the houses I remembered. I'm not even sure why I thought it, but it seemed to feel right.

Look at that house, I said, it looks like Mexico.

Rachel and Lucy look at me like I'm crazy, but before they can let out a laugh, Nenny says: Yes, that's Mexico all right. That's what I was thinking exactly.

Gil's
Furniture
Bought & Sold

There is a junk store. An old man owns it. We bought a used refrigerator from him once, and Carlos sold a box of magazines for a dollar. The store is small with just a dirty window for light. He doesn't turn the lights on unless you got money to buy things with, so in the dark we look and see all kinds of things, me and Nenny. Tables with their feet upside-down and rows and rows of refrigerators with round corners and couches that spin dust in the air when you punch them and a hundred T.V.'s that don't work probably. Everything is on top of everything so the whole store has skinny aisles to walk through. You can get lost easy.

The owner, he is a black man who doesn't talk much and sometimes if you didn't know better you could be in there a long time before your eyes notice a pair of gold glasses floating in the dark. Nenny who thinks she is smart and talks to any old man, asks lots of questions. Me, I never said nothing to him except once when I bought the Statue of Liberty for a dime.

But Nenny, I hear her asking one time how's this here and the man says, This, this is a music box, and I turn around quick thinking he means a *pretty* box with flowers painted on it, with a ballerina inside. Only there's nothing like that where this old man is pointing, just a wood box that's old and got a big brass record in it with holes. Then he starts it up and all sorts of things start happening. It's like all of a sudden he let go a million moths all over the dusty furniture and swan-neck shadows and in our bones. It's like drops of water. Or like marimbas only with a funny little plucked sound to it like if you were running your fingers across the teeth of a metal comb.

And then I don't know why, but I have to turn around and pretend I don't care about the box so Nenny won't see how stupid I am. But Nenny, who is stupider, already is asking how much and I can see her fingers going for the quarters in her pants pocket.

This, the old man says shutting the lid, this ain't for sale.

Meme Ortiz

Meme Ortiz moved into Cathy's house after her family moved away. His name isn't really Meme. His name is Juan. But when we asked him what his name was he said Meme, and that's what everybody calls him except his mother.

Meme has a dog with gray eyes, a sheepdog with two names, one in English and one in Spanish. The dog is big, like a man dressed in a dog suit, and runs the same way its owner does, clumsy and wild and with the limbs flopping all over the place like untied shoes.

Cathy's father built the house Meme moved into. It is wooden. Inside the floors slant. Some rooms uphill. Some down. And there are no closets. Out front there are twenty-one steps, all lopsided and jutting like crooked teeth (made that way on purpose, Cathy said, so the rain will slide off), and when Meme's mama calls from the doorway, Meme goes scrambling up the twenty-one wooden stairs with the dog with two names scrambling after him.

Around the back is a yard, mostly dirt, and a greasy bunch of boards that used to be a garage. But what you remember most is this tree, huge, with fat arms and mighty families of squirrels in the higher branches. All around, the neighborhood of roofs, black-tarred and A-framed, and in their gutters, the balls that never came back down to earth. Down at the base of the tree, the dog with two names barks into the empty air, and there at the end of the block, looking smaller still, our house with its feet tucked under like a cat.

This is the tree we chose for the First Annual Tarzan Jumping Contest. Meme won. And broke both arms.

Louie,
His Cousin &
His Other Cousin

Downstairs from Meme's is a basement apartment that Meme's mother fixed up and rented to a Puerto Rican family. Louie's family. Louie is the oldest in a family of little sisters. He is my brother's friend really, but I know he has two cousins and that his T-shirts never stay tucked in his pants.

Louie's girl cousin is older than us. She lives with Louie's family because her own family is in Puerto Rico. Her name is Marin or Maris or something like that, and she wears dark nylons all the time and lots of makeup she gets free from selling Avon. She can't come out—gotta baby-sit with Louie's sisters—but she stands in the doorway a lot, all the time singing, clicking her fingers, the same song:

Apples, peaches, pumpkin pah-ay.
You're in love and so am ah-ay.

Louie has another cousin. We only saw him once, but it was important. We were playing volleyball in the alley when he drove up in this great big yellow Cadillac with whitewalls and a yellow scarf tied around the mirror. Louie's cousin had his arm out the window. He honked a couple of times and a lot of faces looked out from Louie's back window and then a lot of people came out—Louie, Marin and all the little sisters.

Everybody looked inside the car and asked where he got it. There were white rugs and white leather seats. We all asked for a ride and asked where he got it. Louie's cousin said get in.

We each had to sit with one of Louie's little sisters on our lap, but that was okay. The seats were big and soft like a sofa, and there was a little white cat in the back window whose eyes lit up when the car stopped or turned. The windows didn't roll up like in ordinary cars. Instead there was a button that did it for you automatically. We rode up the alley and around the block six times, but Louie's cousin said he was going to make us walk home if we didn't stop playing with the windows or touching the FM radio.

The seventh time we drove into the alley we heard sirens . . . real quiet at first, but then louder. Louie's cousin stopped the car right where we were and said, Everybody out of the car. Then he took off flooring that car into a yellow blur. We hardly had time to think when the cop car pulled in the alley going just as fast. We saw the yellow Cadillac at the end of the block trying to make a left-hand turn, but our alley is too skinny and the car crashed into a lamppost.

Marin screamed and we ran down the block to where the cop car's siren spun a dizzy blue. The nose of that yellow Cadillac was all pleated like an alligator's, and except for a bloody lip and a bruised forehead, Louie's cousin was okay. They put handcuffs on him and put him in the back-seat of the cop car, and we all waved as they drove away.

Marin

Marin's boyfriend is in Puerto Rico. She shows us his letters and makes us promise not to tell anybody they're getting married when she goes back to P.R. She says he didn't get a job yet, but she's saving the money she gets from selling Avon and taking care of her cousins.

Marin says that if she stays here next year, she's going to get a real job downtown because that's where the best jobs are, since you always get to look beautiful and get to wear nice clothes and can meet someone in the subway who might marry you and take you to live in a big house far away.

But next year Louie's parents are going to send her

back to her mother with a letter saying she's too much trouble, and that is too bad because I like Marin. She is older and knows lots of things. She is the one who told us how Davey the Baby's sister got pregnant and what cream is best for taking off moustache hair and if you count the white flecks on your fingernails you can know how many boys are thinking of you and lots of other things I can't remember now.

We never see Marin until her aunt comes home from work, and even then she can only stay out in front. She is there every night with the radio. When the light in her aunt's room goes out, Marin lights a cigarette and it doesn't matter if it's cold out or if the radio doesn't work or if we've got nothing to say to each other. What matters, Marin says, is for the boys to see us and for us to see them. And since Marin's skirts are shorter and since her eyes are pretty, and since Marin is already older than us in many ways, the boys who do pass by say stupid things like I am in love with those two green apples you call eyes, give them to me why don't you. And Marin just looks at them without even blinking and is not afraid.

Marin, under the streetlight, dancing by herself, is singing the same song somewhere. I know. Is waiting for a car to stop, a star to fall, someone to change her life.

Those Who Don't

Those who don't know any better come into our neighborhood scared. They think we're dangerous. They think we will attack them with shiny knives. They are stupid people who are lost and got here by mistake.

But we aren't afraid. We know the guy with the crooked eye is Davey the Baby's brother, and the tall one next to him in the straw brim, that's Rosa's Eddie V., and the big one that looks like a dumb grown man, he's Fat Boy, though he's not fat anymore nor a boy.

All brown all around, we are safe. But watch us drive into a neighborhood of another color and our knees go shakity-shake and our car windows get rolled up tight and our eyes look straight. Yeah. That is how it goes and goes.

There Was
an Old Woman
She Had
So Many Children
She Didn't Know
What to Do

Rosa Vargas' kids are too many and too much. It's not her fault you know, except she is their mother and only one against so many.

They are bad those Vargases, and how can they help it with only one mother who is tired all the time from buttoning and bottling and babying, and who cries every day for the man who left without even leaving a dollar for bologna or a note explaining how come.

The kids bend trees and bounce between cars and dangle upside down from knees and almost break like fancy museum vases you can't replace. They think it's funny. They are without respect for all things living, including themselves.

But after a while you get tired of being worried about kids who aren't even yours. One day they are playing chicken on Mr. Benny's roof. Mr. Benny says, Hey ain't you kids know better than to be swinging up there? Come down, you come down right now, and then they just spit.

See. That's what I mean. No wonder everybody gave up. Just stopped looking out when little Efren chipped his buck tooth on a parking meter and didn't even stop Refugia from getting her head stuck between two slats in the back gate and nobody looked up not once the day Angel Vargas learned to fly and dropped from the sky like a sugar donut, just like a falling star, and exploded down to earth without even an "Oh."

Alicia
Who Sees Mice

Close your eyes and they'll go away, her father says, or You're just imagining. And anyway, a woman's place is sleeping so she can wake up early with the tortilla star, the one that appears early just in time to rise and catch the hind legs hide behind the sink, beneath the four-clawed tub, under the swollen floorboards nobody fixes, in the corner of your eyes.

Alicia, whose mama died, is sorry there is no one older to rise and make the lunchbox tortillas. Alicia, who inherited her mama's rolling pin and sleepiness, is young and smart and studies for the first time at the university. Two trains and a bus, because she doesn't want to spend her whole life in a factory or behind a rolling pin. Is a good girl, my friend, studies all night and sees the mice, the ones her father says do not exist. Is afraid of nothing except four-legged fur. And fathers.

Darius
& the Clouds

You can never have too much sky. You can fall asleep and wake up drunk on sky, and sky can keep you safe when you are sad. Here there is too much sadness and not enough sky. Butterflies too are few and so are flowers and most things that are beautiful. Still, we take what we can get and make the best of it.

Darius, who doesn't like school, who is sometimes stupid and mostly a fool, said something wise today, though most days he says nothing. Darius, who chases girls with firecrackers or a stick that touched a rat and thinks he's tough, today pointed up because the world was full of clouds, the kind like pillows.

You all see that cloud, that fat one there? Darius said, See that? Where? That one next to the one that look like popcorn. That one there. See that. That's God, Darius said. God? somebody little asked. God, he said, and made it simple.

And Some More

The Eskimos got thirty different names for snow, I say. I read it in a book.

I got a cousin, Rachel says. She got three different names.

There ain't thirty different kinds of snow, Lucy says. There are two kinds. The clean kind and the dirty kind, clean and dirty. Only two.

There are a million zillion kinds, says Nenny. No two exactly alike. Only how do you remember which one is which?

She got three last names and, let me see, two first names. One in English and one in Spanish . . .

And clouds got at least ten different names, I say.

Names for clouds? Nenny asks. Names just like you and me?

That up there, that's cumulus, and everybody looks up.

Cumulus are cute, Rachel says. She *would* say something like that.

What's that one there? Nenny asks, pointing a finger.

That's cumulus too. They're all cumulus today. Cumulus, cumulus, cumulus.

No, she says. That there is Nancy, otherwise known as Pig-eye. And over there her cousin Mildred, and little Joey, Marco, Nereida and Sue.

There are all different kinds of clouds. How many different kinds of clouds can you think of?

Well, there's these already that look like shaving cream . . .

And what about the kind that looks like you combed its hair? Yes, those are clouds too.

Phyllis, Ted, Alfredo and Julie . . .

There are clouds that look like big fields of sheep, Rachel says. Them are my favorite.

And don't forget nimbus the rain cloud, I add, that's something.

Jose and Dagoberto, Alicia, Raul, Edna, Alma and Rickey . . .

There's that wide puffy cloud that looks like your face when you wake up after falling asleep with all your clothes on.

Reynaldo, Angelo, Albert, Armando, Mario . . .

Not my face. Looks like your fat face.

Rita, Margie, Ernie . . .

Whose fat face?

Esperanza's fat face, that's who. Looks like Esperanza's ugly face when she comes to school in the morning.

Anita, Stella, Dennis, and Lolo . . .

Who you calling ugly, ugly?

Richie, Yolanda, Hector, Stevie, Vincent . . .

Not you. Your mama, that's who.

My mama? You better not be saying that, Lucy Guerrero. You better not be talking like that . . . else you can say goodbye to being my friend forever.

I'm saying your mama's ugly like . . . ummm . . .

. . . like bare feet in September!

That does it! Both of yous better get out of my yard before I call my brothers.

Oh, we're only playing.

I can think of thirty Eskimo words for you, Rachel. Thirty words that say what you are.

Oh yeah, well I can think of some more.

Uh-oh, Nenny. Better get the broom. Too much trash in our yard today.

Frankie, Licha, Maria, Pee Wee . . .

Nenny, you better tell your sister she is really crazy because Lucy and me are never coming back here again. Forever.

Reggie, Elizabeth, Lisa, Louie . . .

You can do what you want to do, Nenny, but you better not talk to Lucy or Rachel if you want to be my sister.

You know what you are, Esperanza? You are like the Cream of Wheat cereal. You're like the lumps.

Yeah, and you're foot fleas, that's you.

Chicken lips.

Rosemary, Dalia, Lily . . .

Cockroach jelly.

Jean, Geranium and Joe . . .

Cold *frijoles*.

Mimi, Michael, Moe . . .

Your mama's *frijoles*.
Your ugly mama's toes.
That's stupid.
Bebe, Blanca, Benny . . .
Who's stupid?
Rachel, Lucy, Esperanza, and Nenny.

The
Family
of Little Feet

There was a family. All were little. Their arms were little, and their hands were little, and their height was not tall, and their feet very small.

The grandpa slept on the living room couch and snored through his teeth. His feet were fat and doughy like thick tamales, and these he powdered and stuffed into white socks and brown leather shoes.

The grandma's feet were lovely as pink pearls and dressed in velvety high heels that made her walk with a wobble, but she wore them anyway because they were pretty.

The baby's feet had ten tiny toes, pale and see-through

like a salamander's, and these he popped into his mouth whenever he was hungry.

The mother's feet, plump and polite, descended like white pigeons from the sea of pillow, across the linoleum roses, down down the wooden stairs, over the chalk hop-scotch squares, 5, 6, 7, blue sky.

Do you want this? And gave us a paper bag with one pair of lemon shoes and one red and one pair of dancing shoes that used to be white but were now pale blue. Here, and we said thank you and waited until she went upstairs.

Hurray! Today we are Cinderella because our feet fit exactly, and we laugh at Rachel's one foot with a girl's grey sock and a lady's high heel. Do you like these shoes? But the truth is it is scary to look down at your foot that is no longer yours and see attached a long long leg.

Everybody wants to trade. The lemon shoes for the red shoes, the red for the pair that were once white but are now pale blue, the pale blue for the lemon, and take them off and put them back on and keep on like this a long time until we are tired.

Then Lucy screams to take our socks off and yes, it's true. We have legs. Skinny and spotted with satin scars where scabs were picked, but legs, all our own, good to look at, and long.

It's Rachel who learns to walk the best all strutted in those magic high heels. She teaches us to cross and uncross our legs, and to run like a double-dutch rope, and how to walk down to the corner so that the shoes talk back to you with every step. Lucy, Rachel, me tee-tottering like so. Down to the corner where the men can't take their eyes off us. We must be Christmas.

Mr. Benny at the corner grocery puts down his important cigar: Your mother know you got shoes like that? Who give you those?

Nobody.

Them are dangerous, he says. You girls too young to be wearing shoes like that. Take them shoes off before I call the cops, but we just run.

On the avenue a boy on a homemade bicycle calls out: Ladies, lead me to heaven.

But there is nobody around but us.

Do you like these shoes? Rachel says yes, and Lucy says yes, and yes I say, these are the best shoes. We will never go back to wearing the other kind again. Do you like these shoes?

In front of the laundromat six girls with the same fat face pretend we are invisible. They are the cousins, Lucy says, and always jealous. We just keep strutting.

Across the street in front of the tavern a bum man on the stoop.

Do you like these shoes?

Bum man says, Yes, little girl. Your little lemon shoes are so beautiful. But come closer. I can't see very well. Come closer. Please.

You are a pretty girl, bum man continues. What's your name, pretty girl?

And Rachel says Rachel, just like that.

Now you know to talk to drunks is crazy and to tell them your name is worse, but who can blame her. She is young and dizzy to hear so many sweet things in one day, even if it is a bum man's whiskey words saying them.

Rachel, you are prettier than a yellow taxicab. You know that?

But we don't like it. We got to go, Lucy says.

If I give you a dollar will you kiss me? How about a

dollar. I give you a dollar, and he looks in his pocket for wrinkled money.

We have to go right now, Lucy says taking Rachel's hand because she looks like she's thinking about that dollar.

Bum man is yelling something to the air but by now we are running fast and far away, our high heel shoes taking us all the way down the avenue and around the block, past the ugly cousins, past Mr. Benny's, up Mango Street, the back way, just in case.

We are tired of being beautiful. Lucy hides the lemon shoes and the red shoes and the shoes that used to be white but are now pale blue under a powerful bushel basket on the back porch, until one Tuesday her mother, who is very clean, throws them away. But no one complains.

A
Rice
Sandwich

The special kids, the ones who wear keys around their
necks, get to eat in the canteen. The canteen! Even the
name sounds important. And these kids at lunch time go
there because their mothers aren't home or home is too
far away to get to.

My home isn't far but it's not close either, and some-
how I got it in my head one day to ask my mother to make
me a sandwich and write a note to the principal so I could
eat in the canteen too.

Oh no, she says pointing the butter knife at me as if
I'm starting trouble, no sir. Next thing you know everybody
will be wanting a bag lunch—I'll be up all night cutting

bread into little triangles, this one with mayonnaise, this one with mustard, no pickles on mine, but mustard on one side please. You kids just like to invent more work for me.

But Nenny says she doesn't want to eat at school—ever—because she likes to go home with her best friend Gloria who lives across the schoolyard. Gloria's mama has a big color T. V. and all they do is watch cartoons. Kiki and Carlos, on the other hand, are patrol boys. They don't want to eat at school either. They like to stand out in the cold especially if it's raining. They think suffering is good for you ever since they saw that movie *300 Spartans.*

I'm no Spartan and hold up an anemic wrist to prove it. I can't even blow up a balloon without getting dizzy. And besides, I know how to make my own lunch. If I ate at school there'd be less dishes to wash. You would see me less and less and like me better. Every day at noon my chair would be empty. Where is my favorite daughter you would cry, and when I came home finally at three p.m. you would appreciate me.

Okay, Okay, my mother says after three days of this. And the following morning I get to go to school with my mother's letter and a rice sandwich because we don't have lunch meat.

Mondays or Fridays, it doesn't matter, mornings always go by slow and this day especially. But lunchtime came finally and I got to get in line with the stay-at-school kids. Everything is fine until the nun who knows all the canteen kids by heart looks at me and says: You, who sent you here? And since I am shy, I don't say anything, just hold out my hand with the letter. This is no good, she says, till Sister Superior gives the okay. Go upstairs and see her. And so I went.

I had to wait for two kids in front of me to get hollered at, one because he did something in class, the other because he didn't. My turn came and I stood in front of the big desk with holy pictures under the glass while the Sister Superior read my letter. It went like this:

Dear Sister Superior,
    Please let Esperanza eat in the lunchroom because she lives too far away and she gets tired. As you can see she is very skinny. I hope to God she does not faint.

Thanking you,
Mrs. E. Cordero

You don't live far, she says. You live across the boulevard. That's only four blocks. Not even. Three maybe. Three long blocks away from here. I bet I can see your house from my window. Which one? Come here. Which one is your house?

And then she made me stand up on a box of books and point. That one? she said, pointing to a row of ugly three-flats, the ones even the raggedy men are ashamed to go into. Yes, I nodded even though I knew that wasn't my house and started to cry. I always cry when nuns yell at me, even if they're not yelling.

Then she was sorry and said I could stay—just for today, not tomorrow or the day after—you go home. And I said yes and could I please have a Kleenex—I had to blow my nose.

In the canteen, which was nothing special, lots of boys and girls watched while I cried and ate my sandwich, the bread already greasy and the rice cold.

Chanclas

It's me—Mama, Mama said. I open up and she's there with bags and big boxes, the new clothes and, yes, she's got the socks and a new slip with a little rose on it and a pink-and-white striped dress. What about the shoes? I forgot. Too late now. I'm tired. Whew!

Six-thirty already and my little cousin's baptism is over. All day waiting, the door locked, don't open up for nobody, and I don't till Mama gets back and buys everything except the shoes.

Now Uncle Nacho is coming in his car, and we have to hurry to get to Precious Blood Church quick because that's where the baptism party is, in the basement rented for today for dancing and tamales and everyone's kids running all over the place.

Mama dances, laughs, dances. All of a sudden, Mama is sick. I fan her hot face with a paper plate. Too many tamales, but Uncle Nacho says too many this and tilts his thumb to his lips.

Everybody laughing except me, because I'm wearing the new dress, pink and white with stripes, and new underclothes and new socks and the old saddle shoes I wear to school, brown and white, the kind I get every September because they last long and they do. My feet scuffed and round, and the heels all crooked that look dumb with this dress, so I just sit.

Meanwhile that boy who is my cousin by first communion or something asks me to dance and I can't. Just stuff my feet under the metal folding chair stamped Precious Blood and pick on a wad of brown gum that's stuck beneath the seat. I shake my head no. My feet growing bigger and bigger.

Then Uncle Nacho is pulling and pulling my arm and it doesn't matter how new the dress Mama bought is because my feet are ugly until my uncle who is a liar says, You are the prettiest girl here, will you dance, but I believe him, and yes, we are dancing, my Uncle Nacho and me, only I don't want to at first. My feet swell big and heavy like plungers, but I drag them across the linoleum floor straight center where Uncle wants to show off the new dance we learned. And Uncle spins me, and my skinny arms bend the way he taught me, and my mother watches, and my little cousins watch, and the boy who is my cousin by first communion watches, and everyone says, wow, who are those two who dance like in the movies, until I forget that I am wearing only ordinary shoes, brown and white, the kind my mother buys each year for school.

And all I hear is the clapping when the music stops. My uncle and me bow and he walks me back in my thick shoes to my mother who is proud to be my mother. All night the boy who is a man watches me dance. He watched me dance.

Hips

I like coffee, I like tea.
I like the boys and the boys like me.
Yes, no, maybe so. Yes, no, maybe so . . .

One day you wake up and they are there. Ready and waiting like a new Buick with the keys in the ignition. Ready to take you where?

They're good for holding a baby when you're cooking, Rachel says, turning the jump rope a little quicker. She has no imagination.

You need them to dance, says Lucy.

If you don't get them you may turn into a man. Nenny

says this and she believes it. She is this way because of her age.

That's right, I add before Lucy or Rachel can make fun of her. She is stupid alright, but she *is* my sister.

But most important, hips are scientific, I say repeating what Alicia already told me. It's the bones that let you know which skeleton was a man's when it was a man and which a woman's.

They bloom like roses, I continue because it's obvious I'm the only one who can speak with any authority; I have science on my side. The bones just one day open. Just like that. One day you might decide to have kids, and then where are you going to put them? Got to have room. Bones got to give.

But don't have too many or your behind will spread. That's how it is, says Rachel whose mama is as wide as a boat. And we just laugh.

What I'm saying is who here is ready? You gotta be able to know what to do with hips when you get them, I say making it up as I go. You gotta know how to walk with hips, practice you know—like if half of you wanted to go one way and the other half the other.

That's to lullaby it, Nenny says, that's to rock the baby asleep inside you. And then she begins singing *seashells, copper bells, eevy, ivy, o-ver.*

I'm about to tell her that's the dumbest thing I've ever heard, but the more I think about it . . .

You gotta get the rhythm, and Lucy begins to dance. She has the idea, though she's having trouble keeping her end of the double-dutch steady.

It's gotta be just so, I say. Not too fast and not too slow. Not too fast and not too slow.

We slow the double circles down to a certain speed so Rachel who has just jumped in can practice shaking it.

I want to shake like hoochi-coochie, Lucy says. She is crazy.

I want to move like heebie-jeebie, I say picking up on the cue.

I want to be Tahiti. Or *merengue*. Or electricity.

Or *tembleque!*

Yes, *tembleque*. That's a good one.

And then it's Rachel who starts it:

> *Skip, skip,*
> *snake in your hips.*
> *Wiggle around*
> *and break your lip.*

Lucy waits a minute before her turn. She is thinking. Then she begins:

> *The waitress with the big fat hips*
> *who pays the rent with taxi tips . . .*
> *says nobody in town will kiss her on the lips*
> *because . . .*
> *because she looks like Christopher Columbus!*
> *Yes, no, maybe so. Yes, no, maybe so.*

She misses on maybe so. I take a little while before my turn, take a breath, and dive in:

> *Some are skinny like chicken lips.*
> *Some are baggy like soggy Band-Aids*
> *after you get out of the bathtub.*
> *I don't care what kind I get.*
> *Just as long as I get hips.*

Everybody getting into it now except Nenny who is still humming *not a girl, not a boy, just a little baby*. She's like that.

When the two arcs open wide like jaws Nenny jumps

in across from me, the rope tick-ticking, the little gold earrings our mama gave her for her First Holy Communion bouncing. She is the color of a bar of naphtha laundry soap, she is like the little brown piece left at the end of the wash, the hard little bone, my sister. Her mouth opens. She begins:

> *My mother and your mother were washing clothes.*
> *My mother punched your mother right in the nose.*
> *What color blood came out?*

Not that old song, I say. You gotta use your own song. Make it up, you know? But she doesn't get it or won't. It's hard to say which. The rope turning, turning, turning.

> *Engine, engine number nine,*
> *running down Chicago line.*
> *If the train runs off the track*
> *do you want your money back?*
> *Do you want your MONEY back?*
> *Yes, no, maybe so. Yes, no, maybe so . . .*

I can tell Lucy and Rachel are disgusted, but they don't say anything because she's *my* sister.

> *Yes, no, maybe so. Yes, no, maybe so . . .*

Nenny, I say, but she doesn't hear me. She is too many light-years away. She is in a world we don't belong to anymore. Nenny. Going. Going.

> *Y-E-S spells yes and out you go!*

The First Job

It wasn't as if I didn't want to work. I did. I had even gone to the social security office the month before to get my social security number. I needed money. The Catholic high school cost a lot, and Papa said nobody went to public school unless you wanted to turn out bad.

I thought I'd find an easy job, the kind other kids had, working in the dime store or maybe a hotdog stand. And though I hadn't started looking yet, I thought I might the week after next. But when I came home that afternoon, all wet because Tito had pushed me into the open water hydrant—only I had sort of let him—Mama called me in the kitchen before I could even go and change, and Aunt there drinking her coffee with a spoon. *Lala* ... she had found a job for me at the Peter *Aunt* ...inishers on North Broadway where she *Pan* ... how old was I, and to show up tomorrow *work* ...s one year older, and that was that.

sayi...e next morning I put on the navy blue dress that *ma*...e look older and borrowed money for lunch and *bu*...e because Aunt Lala said I wouldn't get paid till the *ne*...Friday, and I went in and saw the boss of the Peter *p* Photo Finishers on North Broadway where Aunt Lala ...rked and lied about my age like she told me to and sure nough, I started that same day.

In my job I had to wear white gloves. I was supposed to match negatives with their prints, just look at the picture and look for the same one on the negative strip, put it in the envelope, and do the next one. That's all. I didn't know where these envelopes were coming from or where they were going. I just did what I was told.

It was real easy, and I guess I wouldn't have minded it except that you got tired after a while and I didn't know if I could sit down or not, and then I started sitting down only when the two ladies next to me did. After a while they started to laugh and came up to me and said I could sit when I wanted to, and I said I knew.

When lunchtime came, I was scared to eat alone in the company lunchroom with all those men and ladies looking, so I ate real fast standing in one of the washroom stalls and had lots of time left over, so I went back to work early. But then break time came, and not knowing where else to go, I went into the coatroom because there was a bench there.

I guess it was the time for the night shift or middle shift to arrive because a few people came in and punched the time clock, and an older Oriental man said hello and we talked for a while about my just starting, and he said we could be friends and next time to go in the lunchroom and sit with him, and I felt better. He had nice eyes and I didn't feel so nervous anymore. Then he asked if I knew what day it was, and when I said I didn't, he said it was his birthday and would I please give him a birthday kiss. I thought I would because he was so old and just as I was about to put my lips on his cheek, he grabs my face with both hands and kisses me hard on the mouth and doesn't let go.

Papa
Who Wakes Up
Tired
in the Dark

Your *abuelito* is dead, Papa says early one morning in my room. *Está muerto,* and then as if he just heard the news himself, crumples like a coat and cries, my brave Papa cries. I have never seen my Papa cry and don't know what to do.

I know he will have to go away, that he will take a plane to Mexico, all the uncles and aunts will be there, and they will have a black-and-white photo taken in front of the tomb with flowers shaped like spears in a white vase because this is how they send the dead away in that country.

Because I am the oldest, my father has told me first, and now it is my turn to tell the others. I will have to explain why we can't play. I will have to tell them to be quiet today.

My Papa, his thick hands and thick shoes, who wakes up tired in the dark, who combs his hair with water, drinks his coffee, and is gone before we wake, today is sitting on my bed.

And I think if my own Papa died what would I do. I hold my Papa in my arms. I hold and hold and hold him.

Born Bad

Most likely I will go to hell and most likely I deserve to be there. My mother says I was born on an evil day and prays for me. Lucy and Rachel pray too. For ourselves and for each other . . . because of what we did to Aunt Lupe.

Her name was Guadalupe and she was pretty like my mother. Dark. Good to look at. In her Joan Crawford dress and swimmer's legs. Aunt Lupe of the photographs.

But I knew her sick from the disease that would not go, her legs bunched under the yellow sheets, the bones gone limp as worms. The yellow pillow, the yellow smell, the bottles and spoons. Her head thrown back like a thirsty lady. My aunt, the swimmer.

Sandra Cisneros

Hard to imagine her legs once strong, the bones hard and parting water, clean sharp strokes, not bent and wrinkled like a baby, not drowning under the sticky yellow light. Second-floor rear apartment. The naked light bulb. The high ceilings. The light bulb always burning.

I don't know who decides who deserves to go bad. There was no evil in her birth. No wicked curse. One day I believe she was swimming, and the next day she was sick. It might have been the day that gray photograph was taken. It might have been the day she was holding cousin Totchy and baby Frank. It might have been the moment she pointed to the camera for the kids to look and they wouldn't.

Maybe the sky didn't look the day she fell down. Maybe God was busy. It could be true she didn't dive right one day and hurt her spine. Or maybe the story that she fell very hard from a high step stool, like Totchy said, is true.

But I think diseases have no eyes. They pick with a dizzy finger anyone, just anyone. Like my aunt who happened to be walking down the street one day in her Joan Crawford dress, in her funny felt hat with the black feather, cousin Totchy in one hand, baby Frank in the other.

Sometimes you get used to the sick and sometimes the sickness, if it is there too long, gets to seem normal. This is how it was with her, and maybe this is why we chose her.

It was a game, that's all. It was the game we played every afternoon ever since that day one of us invented it— I can't remember who—I think it was me.

You had to pick somebody. You had to think of someone everybody knew. Someone you could imitate and everyone else would have to guess who it was. It started out with famous people: Wonder Woman, the Beatles,

Marilyn Monroe. . . . But then somebody thought it'd be better if we changed the game a little, if we pretended we were Mr. Benny, or his wife Blanca, or Ruthie, or anybody we knew.

I don't know why we picked her. Maybe we were bored that day. Maybe we got tired. We liked my aunt. She listened to our stories. She always asked us to come back. Lucy, me, Rachel. I hated to go there alone. The six blocks to the dark apartment, second-floor rear building where sunlight never came, and what did it matter? My aunt was blind by then. She never saw the dirty dishes in the sink. She couldn't see the ceilings dusty with flies, the ugly maroon walls, the bottles and sticky spoons. I can't forget the smell. Like sticky capsules filled with jelly. My aunt, a little oyster, a little piece of meat on an open shell for us to look at. Hello, hello. As if she had fallen into a well.

I took my library books to her house. I read her stories. I liked the book *The Waterbabies*. She liked it too. I never knew how sick she was until that day I tried to show her one of the pictures in the book, a beautiful color picture of the water babies swimming in the sea. I held the book up to her face. I can't see it, she said, I'm blind. And then I was ashamed.

She listened to every book, every poem I read her. One day I read her one of my own. I came very close. I whispered it into the pillow:

> I want to be
> like the waves on the sea,
> like the clouds in the wind,
> but I'm me.
> One day I'll jump
> out of my skin.

I'll shake the sky
like a hundred violins.

That's nice. That's very good, she said in her tired voice.
You just remember to keep writing, Esperanza. You must
keep writing. It will keep you free, and I said yes, but at
that time I didn't know what she meant.

The day we played the game, we didn't know she was
going to die. We pretended with our heads thrown back,
our arms limp and useless, dangling like the dead. We
laughed the way she did. We talked the way she talked, the
way blind people talk without moving their head. We im-
itated the way you had to lift her head a little so she could
drink water, she sucked it up slow out of a green tin cup.
The water was warm and tasted like metal. Lucy laughed.
Rachel too. We took turns being her. We screamed in the
weak voice of a parrot for Totchy to come and wash those
dishes. It was easy.

We didn't know. She had been dying such a long time,
we forgot. Maybe she was ashamed. Maybe she was em-
barrassed it took so many years. The kids who wanted to
be kids instead of washing dishes and ironing their papa's
shirts, and the husband who wanted a wife again.

And then she died, my aunt who listened to my poems.
And then we began to dream the dreams.

Elenita,
Cards, Palm, Water

Elenita, witch woman, wipes the table with a rag because Ernie who is feeding the baby spilled Kool-Aid. She says: Take that crazy baby out of here and drink your Kool-Aid in the living room. Can't you see I'm busy? Ernie takes the baby into the living room where Bugs Bunny is on T.V.

Good lucky you didn't come yesterday, she says. The planets were all mixed up yesterday.

Her T.V. is color and big and all her pretty furniture made out of red fur like the teddy bears they give away in carnivals. She has them covered with plastic. I think this is on account of the baby.

Yes, it's a good thing, I say.

But we stay in the kitchen because this is where she works. The top of the refrigerator busy with holy candles, some lit, some not, red and green and blue, a plaster saint and a dusty Palm Sunday cross, and a picture of the voodoo hand taped to the wall.

Get the water, she says.

I go to the sink and pick the only clean glass there, a beer mug that says the beer that made Milwaukee famous, and fill it up with hot water from the tap, then put the glass of water on the center of the table, the way she taught me.

Look in it, do you see anything?

But all I see are bubbles.

You see anybody's face?

Nope, just bubbles, I say.

That's okay, and she makes the sign of the cross over the water three times and then begins to cut the cards.

They're not like ordinary playing cards, these cards. They're strange, with blond men on horses and crazy baseball bats with thorns. Golden goblets, sad-looking women dressed in old-fashioned dresses, and roses that cry.

There is a good Bugs Bunny cartoon on T.V. I know, I saw it before and recognize the music and wish I could go sit on the plastic couch with Ernie and the baby, but now my fortune begins. My whole life on that kitchen table: past, present, future. Then she takes my hand and looks into my palm. Closes it. Closes her eyes too.

Do you feel it, feel the cold?

Yes, I lie, but only a little.

Good, she says, *los espíritus* are here. And begins.

This card, the one with the dark man on a dark horse, this means jealousy, and this one, sorrow. Here a pillar of bees and this a mattress of luxury. You will go to a wedding soon and did you lose an anchor of arms, yes, an anchor of arms? It's clear that's what that means.

What about a house, I say, because that's what I came for.

Ah, yes, a home in the heart. I see a home in the heart.

Is that *it*?

That's what I see, she says, then gets up because the kids are fighting. Elenita gets up to hit and then hug them. She really does love them, only sometimes they are rude.

She comes back and can tell I'm disappointed. She's a witch woman and knows many things. If you got a headache, rub a cold egg across your face. Need to forget an old romance? Take a chicken's foot, tie it with red string, spin it over your head three times, then burn it. Bad spirits keeping you awake? Sleep next to a holy candle for seven days, then on the eighth day, spit. And lots of other stuff. Only now she can tell I'm sad.

Baby, I'll look again if you want me to. And she looks again into the cards, palm, water, and says uh-huh.

A home in the heart, I was right.

Only I don't get it.

A new house, a house made of heart. I'll light a candle for you.

All this for five dollars I give her.

Thank you and goodbye and be careful of the evil eye. Come back again on a Thursday when the stars are stronger. And may the Virgin bless you. And shuts the door.

Geraldo
No Last Name

She met him at a dance. Pretty too, and young. Said he worked in a restaurant, but she can't remember which one. Geraldo. That's all. Green pants and Saturday shirt. Geraldo. That's what he told her.

And how was she to know she'd be the last one to see him alive. An accident, don't you know. Hit-and-run. Marin, she goes to all those dances. Uptown. Logan. Embassy. Palmer. Aragon. Fontana. The Manor. She likes to dance. She knows how to do cumbias and salsas and rancheras even. And he was just someone she danced with. Somebody she met that night. That's right.

That's the story. That's what she said again and again.

Once to the hospital people and twice to the police. No address. No name. Nothing in his pockets. Ain't it a shame.

Only Marin can't explain why it mattered, the hours and hours, for somebody she didn't even know. The hospital emergency room. Nobody but an intern working all alone. And maybe if the surgeon would've come, maybe if he hadn't lost so much blood, if the surgeon had only come, they would know who to notify and where.

But what difference does it make? He wasn't anything to her. He wasn't her boyfriend or anything like that. Just another *brazer* who didn't speak English. Just another wetback. You know the kind. The ones who always look ashamed. And what was she doing out at three a.m. anyway? Marin who was sent home with her coat and some aspirin. How does she explain?

She met him at a dance. Geraldo in his shiny shirt and green pants. Geraldo going to a dance.

What does it matter?

They never saw the kitchenettes. They never knew about the two-room flats and sleeping rooms he rented, the weekly money orders sent home, the currency exchange. How could they?

His name was Geraldo. And his home is in another country. The ones he left behind are far away, will wonder, shrug, remember. Geraldo—he went north . . . we never heard from him again.

Edna's Ruthie

Ruthie, tall skinny lady with red lipstick and blue babushka, one blue sock and one green because she forgot, is the only grown-up we know who likes to play. She takes her dog Bobo for a walk and laughs all by herself, that Ruthie. She doesn't need anybody to laugh with, she just laughs.

She is Edna's daughter, the lady who owns the big building next door, three apartments front and back. Every week Edna is screaming at somebody, and every week somebody has to move away. Once she threw out a pregnant lady just because she owned a duck . . . and it was a nice duck too. But Ruthie lives here and Edna can't throw her out because Ruthie is her daughter.

Ruthie came one day, it seemed, out of nowhere. Angel Vargas was trying to teach us how to whistle. Then we heard someone whistling—beautiful like the Emperor's nightingale—and when we turned around there was Ruthie.

Sometimes we go shopping and take her with us, but she never comes inside the stores and if she does she keeps looking around her like a wild animal in a house for the first time.

She likes candy. When we go to Mr. Benny's grocery she gives us money to buy her some. She says make sure it's the soft kind because her teeth hurt. Then she promises to see the dentist next week, but when next week comes, she doesn't go.

Ruthie sees lovely things everywhere. I might be telling her a joke and she'll stop and say: The moon is beautiful like a balloon. Or somebody might be singing and she'll point to a few clouds: Look, Marlon Brando. Or a sphinx winking. Or my left shoe.

Once some friends of Edna's came to visit and asked Ruthie if she wanted to go with them to play bingo. The car motor was running, and Ruthie stood on the steps wondering whether to go. Should I go, Ma? she asked the gray shadow behind the second-floor screen. I don't care, says the screen, go if you want. Ruthie looked at the ground. What do you think, Ma? Do what you want, how should I know? Ruthie looked at the ground some more. The car with the motor running waited fifteen minutes and then they left. When we brought out the deck of cards that night, we let Ruthie deal.

There were many things Ruthie could have been if she wanted to. Not only is she a good whistler, but she can sing and dance too. She had lots of job offers when she was young, but she never took them. She got married instead and moved away to a pretty house outside the city. Only thing I can't understand is why Ruthie is living on Mango Street if she doesn't have to, why is she sleeping on a couch in her mother's living room when she has a real house all her own, but she says she's just visiting and next weekend her husband's going to take her home. But the weekends come and go and Ruthie stays. No matter. We are glad because she is our friend.

I like showing Ruthie the books I take out of the library. Books are wonderful, Ruthie says, and then she runs her hand over them as if she could read them in braille. They're wonderful, wonderful, but I can't read anymore. I get headaches. I need to go to the eye doctor next week. I used to write children's books once, did I tell you?

One day I memorized all of "The Walrus and the Carpenter" because I wanted Ruthie to hear me. "The sun was shining on the sea, shining with all his might . . ." Ruthie looked at the sky and her eyes got watery at times. Finally I came to the last lines: "But answer came there none—and this was scarcely odd, because they'd eaten every one . . ." She took a long time looking at me before she opened her mouth, and then she said, You have the most beautiful teeth I have ever seen, and went inside.

The
Earl of
Tennessee

Earl lives next door in Edna's basement, behind the flower boxes Edna paints green each year, behind the dusty geraniums. We used to sit on the flower boxes until the day Tito saw a cockroach with a spot of green paint on its head. Now we sit on the steps that swing around the basement apartment where Earl lives.

Earl works nights. His blinds are always closed during the day. Sometimes he comes out and tells us to keep quiet. The little wooden door that has wedged shut the dark for so long opens with a sigh and lets out a breath of mold and dampness, like books that have been left out in the rain. This is the only time we see Earl except for when he comes and goes to work. He has two little black dogs that go everywhere with him. They don't walk like ordinary dogs, but leap and somersault like an apostrophe and comma.

At night Nenny and I can hear when Earl comes home from work. First the click and whine of the car door opening, then the scrape of concrete, the excited tinkling of dog tags, followed by the heavy jingling of keys, and finally the moan of the wooden door as it opens and lets loose its sigh of dampness.

Earl is a jukebox repairman. He learned his trade in the South, he says. He speaks with a Southern accent, smokes fat cigars and wears a felt hat—winter or summer, hot or cold, don't matter—a felt hat. In his apartment are boxes and boxes of 45 records, moldy and damp like the smell that comes out of his apartment whenever he opens the door. He gives the records away to us—all except the country and western.

The word is that Earl is married and has a wife somewhere. Edna says she saw her once when Earl brought her to the apartment. Mama says she is a skinny thing, blond and pale like salamanders that have never seen the sun. But I saw her once too and she's not that way at all. And the boys across the street say she is a tall red-headed lady who wears tight pink pants and green glasses. We never agree on what she looks like, but we do know this. Whenever she arrives, he holds her tight by the crook of the arm. They walk fast into the apartment, lock the door behind them and never stay long.

Sire

    I don't remember when I first noticed him looking at me—Sire. But I knew he was looking. Every time. All the time I walked past his house. Him and his friends sitting on their bikes in front of the house, pitching pennies. They didn't scare me. They did, but I wouldn't let them know. I don't cross the street like other girls. Straight ahead, straight eyes. I walked past. I knew he was looking. I had to prove to me I wasn't scared of nobody's eyes, not even his. I had to look back hard, just once, like he was glass. And I did. I did once. But I looked too long when he rode his bike past me. I looked because I wanted to be brave, straight into the dusty cat fur of his eyes and the bike stopped and he bumped into a parked car, bumped, and I walked fast. It made your blood freeze to have somebody look at you like that. Somebody looked at me. Somebody looked. But his kind, his ways. He is a punk, Papa says, and Mama says not to talk to him.

And then his girlfriend came. Lois I heard him call her. She is tiny and pretty and smells like baby's skin. I see her sometimes running to the store for him. And once when she was standing next to me at Mr. Benny's grocery she was barefoot, and I saw her barefoot baby toenails all painted pale pale pink, like little pink seashells, and she smells pink like babies do. She's got big girl hands, and her bones are long like ladies' bones, and she wears makeup too. But she doesn't know how to tie her shoes. I do.

Sometimes I hear them laughing late, beer cans and cats and the trees talking to themselves: wait, wait, wait. Sire lets Lois ride his bike around the block, or they take walks together. I watch them. She holds his hand, and he stops sometimes to tie her shoes. But Mama says those kinds of girls, those girls are the ones that go into alleys. Lois who can't tie her shoes. Where does he take her?

Everything is holding its breath inside me. Everything is waiting to explode like Christmas. I want to be all new and shiny. I want to sit out bad at night, a boy around my neck and the wind under my skirt. Not this way, every evening talking to the trees, leaning out my window, imagining what I can't see.

A boy held me once so hard, I swear, I felt the grip and weight of his arms, but it was a dream.

Sire. How did you hold her? Was it? Like this? And when you kissed her? Like this?

Four Skinny Trees

They are the only ones who understand me. I am the only one who understands them. Four skinny trees with skinny necks and pointy elbows like mine. Four who do not belong here but are here. Four raggedy excuses planted by the city. From our room we can hear them, but Nenny just sleeps and doesn't appreciate these things.

Their strength is secret. They send ferocious roots beneath the ground. They grow up and they grow down and grab the earth between their hairy toes and bite the sky with violent teeth and never quit their anger. This is how they keep.

Let one forget his reason for being, they'd all droop

like tulips in a glass, each with their arms around the other. Keep, keep, keep, trees say when I sleep. They teach.

When I am too sad and too skinny to keep keeping, when I am a tiny thing against so many bricks, then it is I look at trees. When there is nothing left to look at on this street. Four who grew despite concrete. Four who reach and do not forget to reach. Four whose only reason is to be and be.

No Speak English

Mamacita is the big mama of the man across the street, third-floor front. Rachel says her name ought to be *Mamasota*, but I think that's mean.

The man saved his money to bring her here. He saved and saved because she was alone with the baby boy in that country. He worked two jobs. He came home late and he left early. Every day.

Then one day *Mamacita* and the baby boy arrived in a yellow taxi. The taxi door opened like a waiter's arm. Out stepped a tiny pink shoe, a foot soft as a rabbit's ear, then the thick ankle, a flutter of hips, fuchsia roses and green perfume. The man had to pull her, the taxicab driver had to push. Push, pull. Push, pull. Poof!

All at once she bloomed. Huge, enormous, beautiful to look at, from the salmon-pink feather on the tip of her hat down to the little rosebuds of her toes. I couldn't take my eyes off her tiny shoes.

Up, up, up the stairs she went with the baby boy in a blue blanket, the man carrying her suitcases, her lavender hatboxes, a dozen boxes of satin high heels. Then we didn't see her.

Somebody said because she's too fat, somebody because of the three flights of stairs, but I believe she doesn't come out because she is afraid to speak English, and maybe this is so since she only knows eight words. She knows to say: *He not here* for when the landlord comes, *No speak English* if anybody else comes, and *Holy smokes*. I don't know where she learned this, but I heard her say it one time and it surprised me.

My father says when he came to this country he ate hamandeggs for three months. Breakfast, lunch and dinner. Hamandeggs. That was the only word he knew. He doesn't eat hamandeggs anymore.

Whatever her reasons, whether she is fat, or can't climb the stairs, or is afraid of English, she won't come down. She sits all day by the window and plays the Spanish radio show and sings all the homesick songs about her country in a voice that sounds like a seagull.

Home. Home. Home is a house in a photograph, a pink house, pink as hollyhocks with lots of startled light. The man paints the walls of the apartment pink, but it's not the same, you know. She still sighs for her pink house, and then I think she cries. I would.

Sometimes the man gets disgusted. He starts screaming and you can hear it all the way down the street.

Ay, she says, she is sad.

Oh, he says. Not again.

¿Cuándo, cuándo, cuándo? she asks.

¡Ay, caray! We *are* home. This *is* home. Here I am and here I stay. Speak English. Speak English. Christ!

¡Ay! Mamacita, who does not belong, every once in a while lets out a cry, hysterical, high, as if he had torn the only skinny thread that kept her alive, the only road out to that country.

And then to break her heart forever, the baby boy, who has begun to talk, starts to sing the Pepsi commercial he heard on T.V.

No speak English, she says to the child who is singing in the language that sounds like tin. No speak English, no speak English, and bubbles into tears. No, no, no, as if she can't believe her ears.

Rafaela Who Drinks Coconut & Papaya Juice on Tuesdays

On Tuesdays Rafaela's husband comes home late because that's the night he plays dominoes. And then Rafaela, who is still young but getting old from leaning out the window so much, gets locked indoors because her husband is afraid Rafaela will run away since she is too beautiful to look at.

Rafaela leans out the window and leans on her elbow and dreams her hair is like Rapunzel's. On the corner there is music from the bar, and Rafaela wishes she could go there and dance before she gets old.

A long time passes and we forget she is up there watching until she says: Kids, if I give you a dollar will you go to the store and buy me something? She throws a crumpled dollar down and always asks for coconut or sometimes papaya juice, and we send it up to her in a paper shopping bag she lets down with clothesline.

Rafaela who drinks and drinks coconut and papaya juice on Tuesdays and wishes there were sweeter drinks, not bitter like an empty room, but sweet sweet like the island, like the dance hall down the street where women much older than her throw green eyes easily like dice and open homes with keys. And always there is someone offering sweeter drinks, someone promising to keep them on a silver string.

Sally

Sally is the girl with eyes like Egypt and nylons the color of smoke. The boys at school think she's beautiful because her hair is shiny black like raven feathers and when she laughs, she flicks her hair back like a satin shawl over her shoulders and laughs.

Her father says to be this beautiful is trouble. They are very strict in his religion. They are not supposed to dance. He remembers his sisters and is sad. Then she can't go out. Sally I mean.

Sally, who taught you to paint your eyes like Cleopatra? And if I roll the little brush with my tongue and chew it to a point and dip it in the muddy cake, the one in the little red box, will you teach me?

I like your black coat and those shoes you wear, where did you get them? My mother says to wear black so young is dangerous, but I want to buy shoes just like yours, like your black ones made out of suede, just like those. And one day, when my mother's in a good mood, maybe after my next birthday, I'm going to ask to buy the nylons too.

Cheryl, who is not your friend anymore, not since last Tuesday before Easter, not since the day you made her ear bleed, not since she called you that name and bit a hole in your arm and you looked as if you were going to cry and everyone was waiting and you didn't, you didn't, Sally, not since then, you don't have a best friend to lean against the schoolyard fence with, to laugh behind your hands at what the boys say. There is no one to lend you her hairbrush.

The stories the boys tell in the coatroom, they're not true. You lean against the schoolyard fence alone with your eyes closed as if no one was watching, as if no one could see you standing there, Sally. What do you think about when you close your eyes like that? And why do you always have to go straight home after school? You become a different Sally. You pull your skirt straight, you rub the blue paint off your eyelids. You don't laugh, Sally. You look at your feet and walk fast to the house you can't come out from.

Sally, do you sometimes wish you didn't have to go home? Do you wish your feet would one day keep walking and take you far away from Mango Street, far away and maybe your feet would stop in front of a house, a nice one with flowers and big windows and steps for you to climb up two by two upstairs to where a room is waiting for you. And if you opened the little window latch and gave it a shove, the windows would swing open, all the sky would come in. There'd be no nosy neighbors watching, no motorcycles and cars, no sheets and towels and laundry. Only trees and more trees and plenty of blue sky. And you could laugh, Sally. You could go to sleep and wake up and never have to think who likes and doesn't like you. You could close your eyes and you wouldn't have to worry what people said because you never belonged here anyway and nobody could make you sad and nobody would think you're strange because you like to dream and dream. And no one could yell at you if they saw you out in the dark leaning against a car, leaning against somebody without someone thinking you are bad, without somebody saying it is wrong, without the whole world waiting for you to make a mistake when all you wanted, all you wanted, Sally, was to love and to love and to love and to love, and no one could call that crazy.

Minerva
Writes Poems

Minerva is only a little bit older than me but already she has two kids and a husband who left. Her mother raised her kids alone and it looks like her daughters will go that way too. Minerva cries because her luck is unlucky. Every night and every day. And prays. But when the kids are asleep after she's fed them their pancake dinner, she writes poems on little pieces of paper that she folds over and over and holds in her hands a long time, little pieces of paper that smell like a dime.

She lets me read her poems. I let her read mine. She is always sad like a house on fire—always something wrong.

She has many troubles, but the big one is her husband who left and keeps leaving.

One day she is through and lets him know enough is enough. Out the door he goes. Clothes, records, shoes. Out the window and the door locked. But that night he comes back and sends a big rock through the window. Then he is sorry and she opens the door again. Same story.

Next week she comes over black and blue and asks what can she do? Minerva. I don't know which way she'll go. There is nothing *I* can do.

Bums
in the Attic

I want a house on a hill like the ones with the gardens where Papa works. We go on Sundays, Papa's day off. I used to go. I don't anymore. You don't like to go out with us, Papa says. Getting too old? Getting too stuck-up, says Nenny. I don't tell them I am ashamed—all of us staring out the window like the hungry. I am tired of looking at what we can't have. When we win the lottery . . . Mama begins, and then I stop listening.

People who live on hills sleep so close to the stars they forget those of us who live too much on earth. They don't look down at all except to be content to live on hills. They have nothing to do with last week's garbage or fear of rats. Night comes. Nothing wakes them but the wind.

One day I'll own my own house, but I won't forget who I am or where I came from. Passing bums will ask, Can I come in? I'll offer them the attic, ask them to stay, because I know how it is to be without a house.

Some days after dinner, guests and I will sit in front of a fire. Floorboards will squeak upstairs. The attic grumble.

Rats? they'll ask.

Bums, I'll say, and I'll be happy.

Beautiful & Cruel

I am an ugly daughter. I am the one nobody comes for.

Nenny says she won't wait her whole life for a husband to come and get her, that Minerva's sister left her mother's house by having a baby, but she doesn't want to go that way either. She wants things all her own, to pick and choose. Nenny has pretty eyes and it's easy to talk that way if you are pretty.

My mother says when I get older my dusty hair will settle and my blouse will learn to stay clean, but I have decided not to grow up tame like the others who lay their necks on the threshold waiting for the ball and chain.

In the movies there is always one with red red lips who is beautiful and cruel. She is the one who drives the men crazy and laughs them all away. Her power is her own. She will not give it away.

I have begun my own quiet war. Simple. Sure. I am one who leaves the table like a man, without putting back the chair or picking up the plate.

A Smart Cookie

I could've been somebody, you know? my mother says
and sighs. She has lived in this city her whole life. She can
speak two languages. She can sing an opera. She knows
how to fix a T.V. But she doesn't know which subway train
to take to get downtown. I hold her hand very tight while
we wait for the right train to arrive.

She used to draw when she had time. Now she draws
with a needle and thread, little knotted rosebuds, tulips
made of silk thread. Someday she would like to go to the
ballet. Someday she would like to see a play. She borrows
opera records from the public library and sings with velvety
lungs powerful as morning glories.

Today while cooking oatmeal she is Madame Butter-fly until she sighs and points the wooden spoon at me. I could've been somebody, you know? Esperanza, you go to school. Study hard. That Madame Butterfly was a fool. She stirs the oatmeal. Look at my *comadres*. She means Izaura whose husband left and Yolanda whose husband is dead. Got to take care all your own, she says shaking her head.

Then out of nowhere:

Shame is a bad thing, you know. It keeps you down. You want to know why I quit school? Because I didn't have nice clothes. No clothes, but I had brains.

Yup, she says disgusted, stirring again. I was a smart cookie then.

What Sally Said

He never hits me hard. She said her mama rubs lard on all the places where it hurts. Then at school she'd say she fell. That's where all the blue places come from. That's why her skin is always scarred.

But who believes her. A girl that big, a girl who comes in with her pretty face all beaten and black can't be falling off the stairs. He never hits me hard.

But Sally doesn't tell about that time he hit her with his hands just like a dog, she said, like if I was an animal. He thinks I'm going to run away like his sisters who made the family ashamed. Just because I'm a daughter, and then she doesn't say.

Sally was going to get permission to stay with us a little and one Thursday she came finally with a sack full of clothes and a paper bag of sweetbread her mama sent. And would've stayed too except when the dark came her father, whose eyes were little from crying, knocked on the door and said please come back, this is the last time. And she said Daddy and went home.

Then we didn't need to worry. Until one day Sally's father catches her talking to a boy and the next day she doesn't come to school. And the next. Until the way Sally tells it, he just went crazy, he just forgot he was her father between the buckle and the belt.

You're not my daughter, you're not my daughter. And then he broke into his hands.

The
Monkey
Garden

The monkey doesn't live there anymore. The monkey moved—to Kentucky—and took his people with him. And I was glad because I couldn't listen anymore to his wild screaming at night, the twangy yakkety-yak of the people who owned him. The green metal cage, the porcelain table top, the family that spoke like guitars. Monkey, family, table. All gone.

And it was then we took over the garden we had been afraid to go into when the monkey screamed and showed its yellow teeth.

There were sunflowers big as flowers on Mars and thick cockscombs bleeding the deep red fringe of theater curtains. There were dizzy bees and bow-tied fruit flies turning somersaults and humming in the air. Sweet sweet peach trees. Thorn roses and thistle and pears. Weeds like so many squinty-eyed stars and brush that made your ankles itch and itch until you washed with soap and water. There were big green apples hard as knees. And everywhere the sleepy smell of rotting wood, damp earth and dusty hollyhocks thick and perfumy like the blue-blond hair of the dead.

Yellow spiders ran when we turned rocks over and pale worms blind and afraid of light rolled over in their sleep. Poke a stick in the sandy soil and a few blue-skinned beetles would appear, an avenue of ants, so many crusty lady bugs. This was a garden, a wonderful thing to look at in the spring. But bit by bit, after the monkey left, the garden began to take over itself. Flowers stopped obeying the little bricks that kept them from growing beyond their paths. Weeds mixed in. Dead cars appeared overnight like mushrooms. First one and then another and then a pale blue pickup with the front windshield missing. Before you knew it, the monkey garden became filled with sleepy cars.

Things had a way of disappearing in the garden, as if the garden itself ate them, or, as if with its old-man memory, it put them away and forgot them. Nenny found a dollar and a dead mouse between two rocks in the stone wall where the morning glories climbed, and once when we were playing hide-and-seek, Eddie Vargas laid his head beneath a hibiscus tree and fell asleep there like a Rip Van Winkle until somebody remembered he was in the game and went back to look for him.

This, I suppose, was the reason why we went there. Far away from where our mothers could find us. We and a few old dogs who lived inside the empty cars. We made a clubhouse once on the back of that old blue pickup. And besides, we liked to jump from the roof of one car to another and pretend they were giant mushrooms.

Somebody started the lie that the monkey garden had been there before anything. We liked to think the garden could hide things for a thousand years. There beneath the roots of soggy flowers were the bones of murdered pirates and dinosaurs, the eye of a unicorn turned to coal.

This is where I wanted to die and where I tried one day but not even the monkey garden would have me. It was the last day I would go there.

Who was it that said I was getting too old to play the games? Who was it I didn't listen to? I only remember that when the others ran, I wanted to run too, up and down and through the monkey garden, fast as the boys, not like Sally who screamed if she got her stockings muddy.

I said, Sally, come on, but she wouldn't. She stayed by the curb talking to Tito and his friends. Play with the kids if you want, she said, I'm staying here. She could be stuck-up like that if she wanted to, so I just left.

It was her own fault too. When I got back Sally was pretending to be mad . . . something about the boys having stolen her keys. Please give them back to me, she said punching the nearest one with a soft fist. They were laughing. She was too. It was a joke I didn't get.

I wanted to go back with the other kids who were still jumping on cars, still chasing each other through the garden, but Sally had her own game.

One of the boys invented the rules. One of Tito's friends said you can't get the keys back unless you kiss us and Sally pretended to be mad at first but she said yes. It was that simple.

I don't know why, but something inside me wanted to throw a stick. Something wanted to say no when I watched Sally going into the garden with Tito's buddies all grinning. It was just a kiss, that's all. A kiss for each one. So what, she said.

Only how come I felt angry inside. Like something wasn't right. Sally went behind that old blue pickup to kiss the boys and get her keys back, and I ran up three flights of stairs to where Tito lived. His mother was ironing shirts. She was sprinkling water on them from an empty pop bottle and smoking a cigarette.

Your son and his friends stole Sally's keys and now they won't give them back unles she kisses them and right now they're making her kiss them, I said all out of breath from the three flights of stairs.

Those kids, she said, not looking up from her ironing. That's all?

What do you want me to do, she said, call the cops? And kept on ironing.

I looked at her a long time, but couldn't think of anything to say, and ran back down the three flights to the garden where Sally needed to be saved. I took three big sticks and a brick and figured this was enough.

But when I got there Sally said go home. Those boys said leave us alone. I felt stupid with my brick. They all looked at me as if *I* was the one that was crazy and made me feel ashamed.

And then I don't know why but I had to run away. I had to hide myself at the other end of the garden, in the jungle part, under a tree that wouldn't mind if I lay down and cried a long time. I closed my eyes like tight stars so that I wouldn't, but I did. My face felt hot. Everything inside hiccupped.

I read somewhere in India there are priests who can will their heart to stop beating. I wanted to will my blood to stop, my heart to quit its pumping. I wanted to be dead, to turn into the rain, my eyes melt into the ground like two black snails. I wished and wished. I closed my eyes and willed it, but when I got up my dress was green and I had a headache.

I looked at my feet in their white socks and ugly round shoes. They seemed far away. They didn't seem to be my feet anymore. And the garden that had been such a good place to play didn't seem mine either.

Red Clowns

Sally, you lied. It wasn't what you said at all. What he did. Where he touched me. I didn't want it, Sally. The way they said it, the way it's supposed to be, all the storybooks and movies, why did you lie to me?

I was waiting by the red clowns. I was standing by the tilt-a-whirl where you said. And anyway I don't like carnivals. I went to be with you because you laugh on the tilt-a-whirl, you throw your head back and laugh. I hold your change, wave, count how many times you go by. Those boys that look at you because you're pretty. I like to be with you, Sally. You're my friend. But that big boy, where did he take you? I waited such a long time. I waited by the red clowns, just like you said, but you never came, you never came for me.

Sally Sally a hundred times. Why didn't you hear me when I called? Why didn't you tell them to leave me alone? The one who grabbed me by the arm, he wouldn't let me go. He said I love you, Spanish girl, I love you, and pressed his sour mouth to mine.

Sally, make him stop. I couldn't make them go away. I couldn't do anything but cry. I don't remember. It was dark. I don't remember. I don't remember. Please don't make me tell it all.

Why did you leave me all alone? I waited my whole life. You're a liar. They all lied. All the books and magazines, everything that told it wrong. Only his dirty fingernails against my skin, only his sour smell again. The moon that watched. The tilt-a-whirl. The red clowns laughing their thick-tongue laugh.

Then the colors began to whirl. Sky tipped. Their high black gym shoes ran. Sally, you lied, you lied. He wouldn't let me go. He said I love you, I love you, Spanish girl.

Linoleum Roses

Sally got married like we knew she would, young and not ready but married just the same. She met a marshmallow salesman at a school bazaar, and she married him in another state where it's legal to get married before eighth grade. She has her husband and her house now, her pillowcases and her plates. She says she is in love, but I think she did it to escape.

Sally says she likes being married because now she gets to buy her own things when her husband gives her money. She is happy, except sometimes her husband gets angry and once he broke the door where his foot went through, though most days he is okay. Except he won't let her talk on the telephone. And he doesn't let her look out the window. And he doesn't like her friends, so nobody gets to visit her unless he is working.

She sits at home because she is afraid to go outside without his permission. She looks at all the things they own: the towels and the toaster, the alarm clock and the drapes. She likes looking at the walls, at how neatly their corners meet, the linoleum roses on the floor, the ceiling smooth as wedding cake.

The
Three
Sisters

They came with the wind that blows in August, thin as a spider web and barely noticed. Three who did not seem to be related to anything but the moon. One with laughter like tin and one with eyes of a cat and one with hands like porcelain. The aunts, the three sisters, *las comadres*, they said.

The baby died. Lucy and Rachel's sister. One night a dog cried, and the next day a yellow bird flew in through an open window. Before the week was over, the baby's fever was worse. Then Jesus came and took the baby with him far away. That's what their mother said.

Then the visitors came . . . in and out of the little

house. It was hard to keep the floors clean. Anybody who had ever wondered what color the walls were came and came to look at that little thumb of a human in a box like candy.

I had never seen the dead before, not for real, not in somebody's living room for people to kiss and bless themselves and light a candle for. Not in a house. It seemed strange.

They must've known, the sisters. They had the power and could sense what was what. They said, Come here, and gave me a stick of gum. They smelled like Kleenex or the inside of a satin handbag, and then I didn't feel afraid.

What's your name, the cat-eyed one asked.

Esperanza, I said.

Esperanza, the old blue-veined one repeated in a high thin voice. Esperanza . . . a good good name.

My knees hurt, the one with the funny laugh complained.

Tomorrow it will rain.

Yes, tomorrow, they said.

How do you know? I asked.

We know.

Look at her hands, cat-eyed said.

And they turned them over and over as if they were looking for something.

She's special.

Yes, she'll go very far.

Yes, yes, hmmm.

Make a wish.

A wish?

Yes, make a wish. What do you want?

Anything? I said.

Well, why not?

I closed my eyes.

Did you wish already?

Yes, I said.

Well, that's all there is to it. It'll come true.

How do you know? I asked.

We know, we know.

Esperanza. The one with marble hands called me aside. Esperanza. She held my face with her blue-veined hands and looked and looked at me. A long silence. When you leave you must remember always to come back, she said.

What?

When you leave you must remember to come back for the others. A circle, understand? You will always be Esperanza. You will always be Mango Street. You can't erase what you know. You can't forget who you are.

Then I didn't know what to say. It was as if she could read my mind, as if she knew what I had wished for, and I felt ashamed for having made such a selfish wish.

You must remember to come back. For the ones who cannot leave as easily as you. You will remember? She asked as if she was telling me. Yes, yes, I said a little confused.

Good, she said, rubbing my hands. Good. That's all. You can go.

I got up to join Lucy and Rachel who were already outside waiting by the door, wondering what I was doing talking to three old ladies who smelled like cinnamon. I didn't understand everything they had told me. I turned around. They smiled and waved in their smoky way.

Then I didn't see them. Not once, or twice, or ever again.

Alicia & I
Talking
on
Edna's Steps

I like Alicia because once she gave me a little leather purse with the word GUADALAJARA stitched on it, which is home for Alicia, and one day she will go back there. But today she is listening to my sadness because I don't have a house.

You live right here, 4006 Mango, Alicia says and points to the house I am ashamed of.

No, this isn't my house I say and shake my head as if shaking could undo the year I've lived here. I don't belong. I don't ever want to come from here. You have a home, Alicia, and one day you'll go there, to a town you remember, but me I never had a house, not even a photograph . . . only one I dream of.

No, Alicia says. Like it or not you are Mango Street, and one day you'll come back too.

Not me. Not until somebody makes it better.

Who's going to do it? The mayor?

And the thought of the mayor coming to Mango Street makes me laugh out loud.

Who's going to do it? Not the mayor.

A
House
of
My Own

Not a flat. Not an apartment in back. Not a man's house. Not a daddy's. A house all my own. With my porch and my pillow, my pretty purple petunias. My books and my stories. My two shoes waiting beside the bed. Nobody to shake a stick at. Nobody's garbage to pick up after.

Only a house quiet as snow, a space for myself to go, clean as paper before the poem.

Mango
Says
Goodbye
Sometimes

I like to tell stories. I tell them inside my head. I tell them after the mailman says, Here's your mail. Here's your mail he said.

I make a story for my life, for each step my brown shoe takes. I say, "And so she trudged up the wooden stairs, her sad brown shoes taking her to the house she never liked."

I like to tell stories. I am going to tell you a story about a girl who didn't want to belong.

We didn't always live on Mango Street. Before that we lived on Loomis on the third floor, and before that we lived on Keeler. Before Keeler it was Paulina, but what I remember most is Mango Street, sad red house, the house I belong but do not belong to.

I put it down on paper and then the ghost does not ache so much. I write it down and Mango says goodbye sometimes. She does not hold me with both arms. She sets me free.

One day I will pack my bags of books and paper. One day I will say goodbye to Mango. I am too strong for her to keep me here forever. One day I will go away.

Friends and neighbors will say, What happened to that Esperanza? Where did she go with all those books and paper? Why did she march so far away?

They will not know I have gone away to come back. For the ones I left behind. For the ones who cannot out.

CARAMELO

Every summer, Ceyala "Lala" Reyes's large family packs up three cars and drives from Chicago to the Little Grandfather and Awful Grandmother's house in Mexico City. Struggling to find a voice above the boom of her brothers and to understand her place on this or that side of the border, Lala is a shrewd observer of family life. But when she starts telling the Awful Grandmother's life story, grandmother accuses Lala of

exaggerating. Soon, a multigenerational family narrative turns into a whirlwind exploration of storytelling, lies, and life. Like the cherished rebozo, or shawl, that has been passed down through generations of Reyes women, *Caramelo* is alive with the vibrations of history, family, and love.

LOOSE WOMAN

Sandra Cisneros gives us a book of poems with the lilt of Norteño music and the romantic abandon of a hot Saturday night. Celebrating the cataclysms of love and mapping the faultlines in the Mexican-American psyche, *Loose Woman* is by turns bawdy and introspective, flagrantly erotic and unabashedly funny, a work that is both a tour de force and a triumphant outpouring of pure soul.

WOMAN HOLLERING CREEK

Woman Hollering Creek is a story collection of breathtaking range and authority, whose characters give voice to the vibrant and varied life on both sides of the U.S.–Mexican border. From a young girl revealing secrets only an eleven-year-old can know to a witch woman circling above the village on a predawn flight, the women in these stories offer tales of pure discovery, filled with moments of

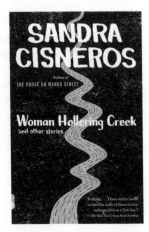

infinite and intimate wisdom. *Woman Hollering Creek* confirms Sandra Cisneros's stature as a writer of electrifying talent.

HAVE YOU SEEN MARIE?

This lyrically told, richly illustrated fable for adults is the tale of a woman's search, in the wake of her mother's death, for a missing cat— and a reminder that love, even when it goes astray, does not stay lost forever.

VINTAGE CISNEROS

In an accessible paperback edition, *Vintage Cisneros* features an excerpt from her bestselling novel *The House on Mango Street*, which has become a favorite in school classrooms across the country. Also included are a chapter from her novel *Caramelo*; a generous selection of poems from *My Wicked Wicked Ways* and *Loose Woman*; and seven stories from her award-winning collection *Woman Hollering Creek*.

Available in Paperback and eBook

Vintage Contemporaries

VintageBooks.com   SandraCisneros.com

ALSO AVAILABLE IN SPANISH

EL ARROYO DE
LA LLORONA

CARAMELO

LA CASA EN
MANGO STREET

¿HAS VISTO A MARÍA?

Available in Paperback and eBook

VintageEspanol.com SandraCisneros.com